KU-621-601

A TOWN
BY THE SEA

Chris Paling

9011277242

Jonathan Cape
London

Published by Jonathan Cape 2005

2 4 6 8 10 9 7 5 3 1

Copyright © Chris Paling 2005

Chris Paling has asserted his right under the Copyright, Designs
and Patents Act 1988 to be identified as the author of this work

This book is sold subject to the condition that it shall not,
by way of trade or otherwise, be lent, resold, hired out,
or otherwise circulated without the publisher's prior
consent in any form of binding or cover other than that
in which it is published and without a similiar condition
including this condition being imposed on the
subsequent purchaser

First published in Great Britain in 2005 by
Jonathan Cape
Random House, 20 Vauxhall Bridge Road, London SW1V 2SA

Random House Australia (Pty) Limited
20 Alfred Street, Milsons Point, Sydney,
New South Wales 2061, Australia

Random House New Zealand Limited
18 Poland Road, Glenfield,
Auckland 10, New Zealand

Random House South Africa (Pty) Limited
Endulini, 5A Jubilee Road, Parktown 2193, South Africa

The Random House Group Limited Reg. No. 954009
www.randomhouse.co.uk

A CIP catalogue record for this book is available from the British Library

ISBN 0-224-07435-0

Papers used by Random House are natural,
recyclable products made from wood grown in sustainable forests;
the manufacturing processes conform to the environmental
regulations of the country of origin

Typeset by Palimpsest Book Production Limited,
Polmont, Stirlingshire
Printed and bound in Great Britain by
Mackays of Chetham plc

For Jim Skinner and Neil Morris

You never enjoy the world aright, till the sea itself floweth in your veins, till you are clothed with the heavens, and crowned with the stars: and perceive yourself to be the sole heir of the whole world, and more than so, because men are in it who are every one sole heirs as well as you.

Thomas Traherne

I

When I awoke the tongue of the tide was lapping at my feet and the sea had claimed my belongings. The sand on which I lay was so stiff there was no trace of my footprints across it. An observer viewing me from above might have imagined I had been washed upon the shore from a shipwreck. Another would perhaps have construed that I had been cast away by choice. If I had encountered my inert body I would have made the former assumption although the latter is much closer to the truth.

I stood with some difficulty; only then, having risen, did I feel the dampness of my clothes. The cold of the sand had not made itself felt while I lay against it. There was no breeze to chill or to dry me. The sun had risen. I could smell salt and a decay which emanated from the tangles of seaweed washed up by the tide. Having lost much of what I owned, I examined what I knew (which was all that remained to me). The month was September. It was a little before seven a.m. I could remember much of the journey that had delivered me here. I knew where it had begun and I could make out some of the features that lay ahead of me. Clearest of all I could see the bleak grey sea and the horizon and the grey sky above it. I counselled myself to dismiss all thoughts of the journey ahead and to concentrate on that moment, that kernel of time. This, I had been assured, would lead me surely to happiness.

'Do not trouble yourself with the hours ahead of you. Regret nothing of the hours that have passed. Only misery lies in contemplating the future.'

When a woman told me this I remember thinking little of it. I rarely pay much heed to what people tell me; I know enough to get by. But when I was next troubled, her words came back to me and I ceased contemplating the day ahead of me. Immediately I felt better. On the following day my misery returned. This time, however, rather than submitting to it, I confronted it. At the heart of the grey cloud was a black, black moment – and that moment was a meeting I had planned, two weeks hence. This was the source of the misery. Before I met the woman I would have accepted the unhappiness but, having unearthed its source, her words granted me a new strength.

So, at a little before seven a.m. in the month of September, on a day that was devoid of any breeze, with my clothes a little wet, my stomach empty, but my heart light, I set out along the beach towards the town which lay some distance to the east of me. It looked a tidy place. There was a greyness about its buildings, but not the drab grey of the sea or the morning sky, it was a vibrant, deep grey which spoke of a proud ancestry of black. Despite the risen sun, lights were lit in the streets. Because their light was superfluous they lent a gay frivolity to the town. As I approached, I could see that the windows were wood-framed and the frames were, without exception, painted in a startling white. Great care had been taken. There was no paint at all on the panes. The housepainter here must, I imagined, be a fully apprenticed man. Not that all the panes were clean. Some were quite smeared with salt spray blown from the sea. The drapes in most of the front rooms were drawn. Those that were not, were clear invitations to passers-by to stand for a while and speculate on the occupation and well-being of those who dwelled there.

I came with some alarm upon a particular room in which a man was asleep at his desk. Beside his elbow was a decanter harbouring a pale gold liquid. A glass stood on the table within reach of his outstretched hand. His forehead was resting upon the pillow of his forearm, his head crowned in grey hair. The hair was thin and his pink scalp clearly visible at the crown. He breathed gently in his sleep; with each inflation his shoulders rose a little before falling again. When I tired of watching him, I surveyed the room. The certificate on the distant wall, the glass-fronted case of books and the chart suggested to me that this was the surgery of the doctor of the town. Perhaps he had been called in the night and, on returning home, had been unable to sleep so had taken refuge here. Doctors are drunkards by and large; it seems also to be the case that most are insomniacs. Drink is what they prescribe themselves in order to sleep. Few, it has always seemed to me, take their own health seriously. Perhaps they feel shame in presenting themselves at the surgeries of their fellow-practitioners because they know that, in the main, few consultations are genuinely required. One visits a doctor generally for reassurance, not for medication. Doctors are lonely creatures.

The man stirred. As he raised his head I saw his face for the first time. It was pained by tiredness. He looked directly towards me but I sensed that he did not see me. Perhaps he was caught in some dream. After a short moment he laid down his head and resumed his slumbers.

Those grey houses with their fine window frames of white fronted a narrow road. On the far side of the road was the promenade. A steep fall beyond it (there was no wall) lay the beach with its wooden breakwaters and gaudy, metal-wheeled bathing machines. When I crossed the road I looked neither left nor right. Despite the advancing hour, the streets were empty. If there was to be life in the town at this hour I felt sure I would find it on the beach. But there was none.

There was, however, in the centre of the promenade, a small metal shelter painted white and emblazoned with the proud, entwined initials of the town's council. The shelter was an elongated letter H. There was a bench at the open front and a matching bench at the back. I sat briefly on the bench facing the town but immediately knew that I was in the wrong place so I stood and made my way to the bench facing the sea. Before I met the woman I am sure that I would have remained on the town bench, too embarrassed to risk being caught out for having made the wrong decision initially. Why this should be I do not know. Perhaps I sense I am undeserving of the space I take up in the world. I know that there are those who consider this to be so. But imagining myself to be under constant observation and feeling undeserving of my place in the world are the twin blights of my life.

Please don't misunderstand me. I am not so foolish as to believe that, had I stood and moved from the town- to the beach-bench, I would have heard someone call, 'Look at that fellow! He chose the wrong bench. Do you see him blush?' But I would have sensed the opprobrium. I'm sure you would argue that this, in itself, is foolish; that the observer and the observed are, in truth, one and the same. But if I truly believed that I lived my life under the constant observation (and disapproval) of myself, then I would feel too wretched to exist. There is one further aspect to this: if I had not first chosen the town-bench then I have the suspicion that I would not have known that the beach-bench was the correct choice. To make progress one must first set out; the direction one initially chooses is unimportant.

I settled myself upon the bench and waited for the day to begin. After almost an hour in which nobody stirred, I chanced a look behind me. This was not an unselfconscious movement. If I had merely turned, as a theatregoer would to one in the row behind, and I had been observed, then the observer could have believed that, again, I was examining the possibility of returning to the town-bench. Instead, I pivoted my head from one side to another, as though I was experiencing some stiffness in the neck. I then turned my head first a little way to the right, then a little way to the left. Having released some of the stiffness, I considered I had then earned the right to turn my head as far as my neck would allow to the left, allowing me an unimpeded view through the glass partition at the side of the shelter towards the heart of the town.

Beyond the grey houses was a terrace of shops, each of which had a colourful canvas awning extended over the pavement in front of it. A veil of mist hung about them. In the third shop of the row I saw a woman busying herself bringing out a number of weathered wicker baskets of wooden-handled spades, tin buckets, green shrimp nets, and other beach paraphernalia. She seemed content in her work, disappearing into the dark door of the shop, each time to

6

emerge with another basket. Having satisfied myself with my inventory of the woman's goods, I turned my attention to her. She was young and wore loose-fitting clothes. Her hair was fair and fine and long and I saw contentment in her face. Her eyes sang with joy, her body was free in its movement. I considered whether or not I should approach her but there was little in her stock that suggested itself as a suitable topic for conversation. Perhaps the spades would suffice: do they, perhaps, give her any trouble by rusting in the salt breeze? No, this would have seemed far too ludicrous an opening: I did not want to appear a madman and be driven out of the town. Instead, I determined to approach her and wait for a thought to occur to me. Such a strategy has rewarded me in the past, although sometimes I have waited for too long and been judged mentally deficient. People, I have found, are quick to make such judgments. If one does not conform to their expectations (which are largely dictated by their own behaviour), one is marked out as being mentally wanting. But I craved human contact. I could sense my time was drawing near. I had come to this town for a reason and if I was to succeed then it was necessary for me to begin to ask the questions that would lead me to my destination.

I felt the momentary sadness come over me. It is a familiar feeling and one which attends each arrival and prefigures each new departure.

I stood and stretched. This was only a partly contrived gesture. I needed to stretch as one often does, and therefore I did. The woman saw me. She seemed a little taken aback to find the shelter inhabited at this early hour. I did not yet know the town sufficiently well to understand the etiquette. In other places, in other cities and towns, there are roads it is unwise to walk down, there are places at the bar counter where one should not stand, squares and alleys it is foolhardy to visit after dark. There are, in short, conventions the traveller must quickly learn before he earns acceptance.

In one dark city (where all of the buildings were made of wood) there was a clock which chimed once a day. The chime was preceded by the opening of two doors at the top of the tall tower. Through the doors there emerged two mechanical buglers which sailed out on metal tracks. When each reached an equivalent point in the tracks, a device triggered their right arms to raise the bugles to their mouths. As each did so, the clock would chime. I mention this only because it was the single moment of the day in which all of the city dwellers in the vicinity came out of their shops and businesses and stood still and silent to watch the chime. The visitors were therefore immediately identifiable by the fact that they continued to move about and talk to each other. The city dwellers watched them with disdain; in its way the behaviour was quite shocking. Because

I stood in silence among them I sensed that they accepted me, and when I moved on I carried this acceptance with me.

I timed my approach to the woman badly. I had hoped to arrive at her shop just as she emerged from the door. I could therefore have greeted her as though each of us had, by some happy coincidence, arrived at the same part of the world at the same time. I have often wondered why we do not greet each other with more assiduity. After all, the odds of two souls meeting at any point in the world (unless by prior arrangement) are so long that we should greet every stranger with delight. The streets should resound with cries of welcome, with backslapping; hands being firmly shaken. By the time I arrived at the shop, however, the woman had returned inside and I feared that she had concluded her morning tasks and retired to her place behind the counter. I could not find the courage to enter, implicating me, as it would have done, to some extent in a commercial transaction I did not have the means to conclude. No. If we were to talk then it was necessary for her to come out of the shop one more time. And immediately she did, and because she was who she was – and was not burdened as I was – and, seemingly without any contemplation of the consequences, she greeted me.

'Good morning!' I imagined these words to be. I knew I had done right to come to this town.

9

What else could I reply but, 'And good morning to you!' This was just as I had hoped it would be. The impetus now lay with her to continue. All that was now required of me was to follow her lead.

I waited. And I waited a little longer. The woman continued to look straight at me, but it was as if she no longer saw me. As if, indeed, I was a trick of the light. Her brow furrowed. It struck me that perhaps she had not understood my response so I repeated the greeting, but she turned away from me and made a step back towards the sanctuary of the shop. Muttering a word beneath her breath, she hurried inside, pulling the door shut behind her.

The door was glass-paned. In it I could see something of my reflection, though in the exchange I had been robbed of my substance. Had my black coat, my pallid complexion, my dark hair, tangled and salty from my night on the beach, intimidated her? I examined my appearance and concluded that in a town such as this, perhaps she did take me for a vagabond whose intention was to rob her as she opened up her shop. But if this was the case, then why did she greet me initially with such warmness? I approached the door. There was nothing for it but to confront her. I was no longer in any doubt as to the way the conversation should proceed. My uncertainty was vanquished. I tried the knob and it turned but when I pushed at the door it did not budge. Perhaps the frame had swollen. I pushed harder but the door was locked.

I peered inside at the brown-shadowed shapes on the shelves. There was no artificial light, just a little miserly illumination borrowed from the early sun. I could make out very little among the shadows. If the woman was there then she was standing very still. I touched my palm to the door and absorbed the chill of the glass. When I drew it away, my palm clung briefly to the pane as if the glass that had reflected me wanted to pull me inside and imprison me. At the same moment I caught a whiff of dampness, perhaps even of rot, from the building itself. There was a small movement inside. It seemed that the woman had not gone through to the back of the shop. Instead she was waiting inside, watching me. In turn, I watched her. My eyes accustomed themselves to the dimness of the interior of the shop. Shapes sharpened. On the counter I saw boxes of glass marbles, greedy for the light. On the shelves behind I saw tall glass jars of liquorice and twisted sugar candies, bull's-eyes and tangles of sugared seaweed. Between the counter and the shelves stood the woman.

When she saw that I had seen her she made a pretence of tidying up the papers on the shop counter. This took very little time and I could see that she regretted having wasted the opportunity to busy herself. She drew in a breath and then expelled it, placing her knuckles on the counter.

11

All of this activity was to delay her from returning to the door and unlocking it. I was grateful that she was taking so much trouble over me. I was a stranger, what did she know of me? Well, clearly, I reflected, she knew enough to engage in this unnecessary activity so that my feelings would not be hurt by her choosing not to unlock the door. Already we had reached a moment of intimacy, perhaps even tenderness. But her knuckled hands suggested to me that she was embarrassed at being watched. I recognised the condition. When we are alone and unobserved our arms and our hands are no encumbrance. But in company, as the practised liar knows, our limbs (yes, our legs also) often serve to contradict our words. A good lie demands control of the voice, the face and the entire body. From the evidence that the woman had bunched her knuckles, I understood that she was feeling some aggression. But the fingers, clenched tight into fists, were directed back towards her. She was angry with herself; angry because she knew now she should not have locked the door.

As conversations go, I was beginning to enjoy my time with the shop woman. Already we had enough in common to suggest that we could be friends (although I have found in the past that similarities often repel).

After she had taken in and expelled a further breath, which ruffled her fine hair, she fanned her face with her slender hand. She was signalling to me that soon she would go behind her curtain for water. At that point I would lose her entirely and I think she knew this, which was why she did not immediately remove herself from my sight. Something held her, some promise our brief acquaintance had made. What to do? Her inactivity had returned the impetus to me. This was why she waited. What I chose to do next would dictate whether or not she went away through the curtain. What could I do? I could call or I could knock; I could take three steps back in the hope that curiosity would draw her towards the door; I could duck down and vanish, and hope that this would achieve the same effect. Or I could sing — and surely a song was the last thing she expected to hear from me on such a September morning. I could think of no better reason. But just as I came to this decision she raised her eyes from the papers on the counter and looked towards me: a clear challenge; my final chance.

I licked my lips and tasted salt and then I began. At first my voice was gentle, like water, but when I had judged my pitch — loud enough for her to hear, not so loud as to wake the neighbourhood — I gave it full rein. The song concerned a dog which had been abandoned by its master beneath a bridge. The master was too poor to feed it and had chosen the bridge because it would provide the dog with shelter. However, each time the master walked away the loyal dog would follow him. To prevent this, the man tied the dog with rope to a metal hoop secured in the damp brickwork of the bridge. The dog followed him to the extent of the rope but could then only watch and bark sadly as the man deserted him. That night it rained hard. The river rose. In the morning the towpath beneath the bridge was submerged beneath the water. There was no sign of the dog. The master was distraught. Already unbalanced by hunger, this pushed him beyond sanity. He returned home, and once there he stood on a stool and secured a further length of the rope to a rafter in the ceiling. He took a final look around his poor room before kicking away the stool. The rope bit into his throat and began to choke him, but he had not, as all good suicides know to, tied the knot in such a way as to break his neck. Instead, he thrashed about, dancing in the air. The rope broke and he fell to the floor. The last verse finds him rolling about in mirth on the floor of his room while the dog is heard to be barking outside.

Although the woman was still staring towards me, the focus of her gaze had shifted and she was now looking into herself. The shop door and my shape beyond it had become a canvas on to which she was painting her interpretation of the story. She curtailed her thoughts with a sharp nod and strode over to the door. I heard the key turn and prepared myself for the discussion ahead: why did the man laugh? Was he a fully fledged lunatic? I had held this conversation (with myself and others) many times. The door opened and the woman came out into the sun which had now broken through the mist and was shining brightly. Her eyes shrank momentarily, as if in response to a sharp pain. Out of politeness I took a step back; I did not want to crowd her. But she proceeded straight past me without a word or a look of acknowledgment. And then, rather than returning to her baskets, she set off along the street leaving me in sole charge of the shop. She walked in long, graceful strides. I had misjudged her height. She was half a foot taller than I.

Another test? I had hoped this would be the end of it. But I was exhausted now. She had defeated me and I was at her mercy.

I stepped into the shop with trepidation, imagining how I would feel if I had entered it as a customer might. A little afraid, I believe, particularly had I been a child. The dimness menaced the goods boxed upon the shelves and the bottled sweets behind the counter. It dampened the appetite for life, bidding one towards sleep. This was not the convivial setting one requires to part with money. Although the shop woman was gone, her presence remained a ghost in the room. The papers, neatened by her hand, remained neatened. There was a small indentation in one pile where her knuckles had lain. I could smell the soap she had used to wash herself that morning, and could differentiate a lighter, sweeter fragrance that had been employed on her clothes.

It was then that I heard a movement in the room above. Why I had assumed that the woman lived alone I do not know, but she did not have the demeanour of a married woman. There was no suggestion of a fellow weighing down her shoulders, she carried herself too straight. And neither had she called out to explain that she was leaving the shop. Perhaps there was a lesser burden in the household: an aged parent, or lover, or perhaps even a child.

Although the movement above me had now ceased, my curiosity was such that it impelled me to move behind the counter. I was glad of a reason to leave the grim shop. If the woman returned and found me in the room upstairs I would explain that I had heard a call for help. I pushed through the beaded curtain (which was heavier than I had anticipated), but paused with the curtain about me as if caught by a photographer in a hailstorm. Each bead, I discovered, was a joy in itself. I grasped a handful and let them fall through my fingers; they were cool and of a great weight. I pressed on, and on the other side I found a small hallway. Off to the left was an unlit storeroom. Immediately ahead of me was a set of open wooden steps such as one might find in the cellar of a bar. They rose steeply to the floor above. The damp and decay I had first smelled outside the shop was stronger here and seemed to emanate from the storeroom. I hurried past it, feeling a shiver pass up my spine.

Once on the steps I found that I must climb them as I would have climbed a ladder, they were too steep to use as a staircase. I grasped the rails on each side, cautious of splinters, and made my way up. My head arriving at the upper landing, I paused and looked around me. I was confronted by a short corridor with a door to the left and a door to the right. At the far end was anchored the base of a further set of narrow wooden steps which returned towards me, making a triangle of the space on the right side of the landing. Looking above me, I saw a trapdoor at the top of the steps. I then completed my climb with agility, brushed the dust from my hands and stood silently, listening. There was no sound from the room to the right of me, nor from the room to the left. Both the doors were closed and each was latched in the old style. I knocked on the door to my left. There was no reply. I did the same to the door on my right. Again, no reply. Boldly, I unlatched the door (for some obscure reason removing my hat as I did so). I called a greeting and walked into the room. It was empty, save for a bed, a chair, a washstand and a basin. At first sight, therefore, there was nothing at all remarkable about the room. However, when I went over to the small window and tried to peer out, I saw that the walls of the room were noticeably curved. Further, that the window was set some three or four feet into what proved to be a most substantial wall, making for a considerable width of ledge. This suggested to me that the dimensions of the building were more akin to a castle keep than a commercial premises. I took myself to the other room. Again with my hat in my left hand, I knocked, waited and entered. The room was sparse. At the centre of the bare floorboards there stood a square wood table with four chairs drawn tight in to each side of it. A chandelier hung above it which provided the sole decoration, although its grandeur mocked the simplicity of the room it reigned over. There were no paintings on the bare, distempered curving walls. The window ahead of me was set back in similar fashion to that of the bedroom.

I was puzzled. From the outside (although I had made only a cursory glance) I had assumed that the shop, like the row of dwellings which ran up to it, was square and flat-fronted and that, above it, there was a tidy roof. But had I, indeed, made this assumption after approaching the shop from the houses to the west of it, and had the formality of the terrace tricked me into a false assumption? If the walls were curved this surely argued that the building was not square but circular and that the two walls at each end of the hallway were therefore, perhaps, also curved. I returned to the landing but found the walls to be dead straight. There remained the possibility that there was a hidden, semicircular room behind each of the end walls of the hallway, access to which was by another route. The circular building (I had ceased now to think of it merely as a shop) would therefore have been perhaps forty feet in diameter, with thick walls and, presumably, solid foundations set deep below the level of the shop floor and the storeroom. But was I now at the top of the building, or simply part-way up? All thoughts of the woman and my responsibilities towards tending the counter had now deserted me. I was full of curiosity about the building, sensing, as I did, that fate had brought me here for a purpose.

In my mind I took myself back to my approach to the terrace and retraced my steps. After seeing the doctor asleep at his desk I had turned my attention to the sea. When I had taken my seat in the shelter on the promenade I had been so exercised by moving to the beach-seat that I had paid scant attention to the shops and the town ahead of me. When, finally, I had approached the woman setting out her baskets, my only concern had been what I would say to her. Would I have noticed anything above? Perhaps not, particularly had the mist been thick. But why was I wasting my time examining what I had anticipated? I had been presented with two options: to climb further or to go back outside and survey the building from there. I hope that you know me sufficiently well by now to know which course I took. In under a minute I was at the top of the next set of steps and standing at the centre of a circular room. This chamber had no walls to partition it, no furniture, simply bare brick walls with two windows set into them. Access to it had been through a trapdoor which suddenly dropped shut behind me to an enormous echo that bounded glee-fully around the walls.

My assumption had been correct. The diameter of the building was, indeed, approximately forty feet. What differ-entiated this floor from the last was the height of the ceiling. Whereas the previous one had been perhaps nine or ten feet high, this time the boards were seven or eight feet above my head. And any notion that this was the end of my climb was immediately dispelled, for this time a wooden ladder led to a square trap in the ceiling above. By now I had concluded that it would be prudent to make an assessment of the task ahead of me, determined, as I was, to reach the top of the tower (and when I reached the top I would assess whether tower was an appropriate descrip-tion). I therefore returned to the trapdoor with a view to climbing down the two sets of steps, leaving the building through the shop and taking up a vantage point on the promenade. From there, the mist having lifted, the height of the tower would be immediately apparent. The trap-door, however, was impossible to raise. Despite the rope attached to it, the size of it (four feet square) and the depth

of it (five or six inches) made it too heavy for one man to
lift. I attempted this a number of times, believing that if
I took it by surprise perhaps I would catch gravity napping
and could snatch it open before it awoke. I succeeded only
in wrenching a muscle just below my right shoulderblade.

At this moment, as I circled the room like a mule at a
well, I found that my excitement at the task ahead had
palled, the joyous child of my hope cowering now before
the monster of despair. I had neither food nor water. Not
having eaten for more than a day, my hunger now cried
out. I paused at the window recess. I reasoned that if I
could open the window then perhaps I could alert a passer-
by on the promenade. Two or three men could raise the
trapdoor from below and I would be free. I felt stronger
as I pushed my head and shoulders into the narrow aperture that led to the window. Pulling myself along it with
my fingers and shrugging with my shoulders, my nose was
soon at the thick green glass of the pane. Regrettably, there
had never been any intention for this window to be opened.
There was no frame, the glass being set directly into the
surrounding brickwork. My body was so constricted by the
space that all I could do was test the strength of the pane
with my forehead. It was as cold and strong as steel. Nor
could I see below me to the promenade and thus I could
not enjoy the small reassurance of people going about their
daily lives. All that lay within my sight was the grey sea,

huge and malevolent, waiting to menace anyone foolhardy enough to set sail on it.

I slid backwards and out again into the room, grateful for the mercy of the space around me again. I strode over to the ladder, tested its strength, and climbed. Soon I had reached the floor above.

One can live many lives in an hour. With each life the birth of new hope. But I died many deaths that day as I climbed that tower. And as I climbed, the sun slowly moved above me. By the middle of the day I was entering chambers deep in shadow; as the afternoon wore on, each new floor was light again, which lifted my spirits. But by six p.m. the sun had dropped away and I knew that I was destined to spend the night cold and dark and afraid.

I continued to climb even when dusk came. So practised was I that I could have proceeded with my eyes shut, for each floor was identical, although the higher I climbed, the colder it became. Only once did I pause, when I glimpsed a black shape pass a window. Another followed, then another. I made my way to the pane and watched as several birds circled the tower. They were large, their feathers a glossy, regal black, their black-beaded eyes harbouring a cold intelligence. I had no doubt that they knew I was there, watching them. I rested, trying to gain some reassurance from the proximity of the cold circling creatures.

But there was no kinship between us. Which made us enemies, not friends.

When, long into the night, I could go no further, I lay down and slept.

2

My senses rarely awaken together. Sometimes my ears rouse my eyes from slumber; a sound has been heard, are we in danger? More usually it is the light of day which my eyes acknowledge, my other senses grumblingly awakening shortly afterwards. But rarely am I awakened by an aroma so rich that I lie, eyes closed, consuming it: apples. And until I opened my eyes I could enjoy the pretence that a barrel of apples had appeared in the night, which could satisfy the demands of both my hunger and my thirst. Finally I could bear it no longer. I sat up and looked around me. There was no barrel on the floor, nor was there now any smell of apples. I had carried the hope of sustenance with me from a dream. The dream was of interest to me for it represented (within its own logic) a period of time in which I served in an army. Isolated in the tower, I was seeking companionship in my past. My role in the army had been that of a mascot rather than a fighter. Various men had attempted to teach me the rudiments of shooting a pistol but the noise and recoil of each discharge made the weapon leap like a fish from my shaking hand.

The dream concerned a man I knew only as the fool. In recounting it my apologies are offered, for removed from the scaffolding of our experience, dreams often collapse into meaninglessness.

The fool and I are in an orchard, in the broken-walled garden of a large ruined villa. We are standing beside an oval of mud which is all that remains of an unshaded pond. The gardener is dead, the forsythia already overgrown, a chestnut tree untended. A metal sundial has been removed from its plinth and now lies on the ground. The sun has bleached the circle it left behind on the stone. The terracotta-tiled roof of the villa has slipped and has taken on the appearance of a hat with its brim turned down over the windows of its eyes.

'If you are thirsty you may do this,' the fool begins, planting his right sandal into the mud before lifting it again. Brown water slowly floods the footprint. He kneels and scoops the water into his palms before it seeps back into the ground. As he lifts his cupped hands to his mouth a muddy goatee appears upon his chin.

'How does it taste?' I ask him.

'Like . . . like wine.' The fool licks his lips and rubs his firm belly. 'It is making me drunk.' He shouts to the men seeking shade from the wall. 'This water is so good it is making me drunk! Try some yourselves before it dries up.'

A stone hurled by a weary infantryman narrowly misses his head. The fool scurries after it and to nobody's amusement throws it high into the air. Watching its trajectory he takes two steps backwards, shields his eyes against the sun and adjusts his position to ensure that the falling stone strikes him squarely on the crown of his head. He then clutches his heart and dies a long-drawn-out death in the mud. The twenty or so men close by who are trying to rest are tired of his antics. I take the fool's hand and pull him to his feet.

'They don't know what I know,' the fool says, slyly.

'And what do you know?' I ask him as I lead him away.

'I know many things. I know how to juggle three wooden hoops while balancing a chair on my chin.'

'But what do you know about the war?'

'I know nothing about the war.'

I recall that I have been trying to free myself from the fool's attention since the man arrived with a new squadron two days before.

'But I do know that the Generalissimo is waiting for the city to empty before he marches in.'

'And how do you know that?'

'A man told me who was hiding behind a wall.'

'A wall?'

'Yes, a man was speaking about the Generalissimo behind

a wall. A very deep-voiced man. And I wondered what the man was doing there and I wanted to ask him to come out from behind the wall and tell everybody what he knew because he seemed to know so much. So I climbed the wall and sat across the top and do you know what I saw?'

'No.'

'A wooden box. On a chair. And the man imprisoned inside the box — although the box seemed too small for such a purpose.'

'. . . You were telling me about the city. Why will the city empty?'

'Because the men are cowards and will run away. The Generalissimo in his wisdom and generosity demands that these misguided souls have a chance to flee before we march victorious into the city. I, personally, will lead the parade astride a beautiful Andalusian stallion which I will ride facing backwards. As we enter the city I will perform a handstand on the flanks. I will then vault from the horse and do cartwheels to draw the attention of the cheering crowds. In this way, if the enemy have left any men behind to assassinate the Generalissimo, I will draw their fire.'

The fool's lucidity, I had come to learn, was determined by the time of day. He became light-headed and more foolish with hunger. After he had eaten he quietened, and often fell asleep. A brief sleep, however, charged him with energy which he began to expend immediately upon awakening. I recognised something of my youthful self in the man's behaviour. He would abase himself in any way he could to earn a smile or a laugh. His face was that of a clown or a brutalised dog, his pain or pleasure conveyed by his eyes. The fool was thirty-three years old and seemed to have earned a living variously from clowning, tumbling, singing, writing and reciting poetry and, where necessary, labouring. He had attached himself to the squadron in a place called Melilla, where he said he had gone to look for gold bars under the Moroccan sand.

'What else did you hear?' I ask him.

'I heard . . . what did I hear? Yes, my good friend, my pretty boy, I heard that the army are packing the treasures from the museum into wooden crates and transporting them to a port in the east. From there they will be attached by chains to huge birds and flown across the sea and we will never see them again.' The fool performs a handstand and the legs of his loose brown breeches concertina around his tanned and muscular thighs. Upended, he finds a point of equilibrium, his legs bend a little at the knee and he begins to walk away from me on his hands. When he reaches the wall he pauses, gathers his strength, lowers his shoulders and somehow launches himself into the air, clapping his hands once before he plants them on the ground again. With another jump he has completed a full circle and now begins to walk back on his hands towards me. The men in the shade of the wall are watching him with more interest. One of them thumbs a spinning coin towards him. It flashes in the sun and drops into the dirt. When the fool reaches it he lowers his head to the ground and picks it up with his teeth. His strength, the men acknowledge, is prodigious and has saved him from a number of beatings.

When he reaches me the fool slowly, with great control, lowers his feet to the ground. He stands, rubs the dust from his hands, and bows like a dancer, delicately crossing his wrists against his heart then whipping his arms wide, his head staying down. Finally, shyly, his head remaining low, he lifts his eyes towards his audience. His expression offers little indication as to what he expects. One or two of the men have begun to suspect that the joke may be on them.

'You look sad, my friend,' the fool says, another character now: the clown has become a wiser, older man, crossing his legs at the ankles and lowering himself, without the use of his hands, straight-backed, to sit beside me. He takes my right hand in his and traces the lines in my palm. 'This hand, the last city. Yes?'

'I don't understand.' I am miserable and hungry and tired, but the fool will not let me rest. In his company I feel my loyalty is being tested. Many of the fool's questions, like those of my mother, are tainted by an expectation of the answer. 'Why is my hand the last city?' I ask impatiently.

30

'You did not hear about the fortress?'

'No. Nobody speaks to me.'

'Poor, poor boy. Well I am speaking to you now of two days past when my friends and I came from an ancient Arab fortress . . . here.' The fool rubs the mound at the base of my thumb. 'Your soft hand is the last city. The tiny mound is the fortress. You see? Fortress, thumb; city, palm.'

'Yes.'

'When the movement began it was our misfortune that the enemy triumphed in the last city and many who were sympathetic to our cause — officers, guards, some cadets — took refuge in the fort. They pulled the gates closed after them and they stood on the ramparts and shot at the soldiers around them. Bang, bang, bang. The fortress walls were so thick that the enemy, although they tried, couldn't push them over. Now, you might ask me why did they not then bring up a cannon and immediately begin to blast the walls down? . . . I'll tell you why. Because the men had taken four hundred women and children into the fortress with them. They simply knocked on the doors of the last city and asked the women and children to go with them. Of course some of them refused, but those who did were carried in on the shoulders of the gentle soldiers. Think of it! Four hundred wives and children of the enemy who were outside! What a puzzle. What a terrible puzzle for them as the days went on and nothing was heard from inside . . . what could they do?' Having posed the question, the fool falls sideways to the ground and feigns sleep by snoring loudly.

'What did they do?' I ask, shaking the fool's shoulder.

'Please don't wake me.'

'Tell me. What did they do?'

'Dawn already?' The fool stretches his arms, yawns and sits upright. 'Well. They waited for a day. And another day. And finally a week had passed. Two weeks. Three. Four. And all the time they waited, we marched closer and closer to them, conquering all as we advanced. We were told that the smell from the fortress began to make the men outside the walls sick. The stench was the dead horses within the walls that those imprisoned were eating. Did I tell you that they had a little bran for bread but no more food and not much clean water? The disease was unimaginable . . . After seventy days we arrived and liberated the brave hostages of the fortress.'

'You saved the children? And the women?'

'Ah . . . that is a question for my friends I think.' The fool looks towards the men beneath the wall. Many are asleep on the ground using their packs to rest their heads. Tripods have been formed of their rifles. 'When I was alone I wandered into a militia barracks close by the fortress. I met many ghosts. On a wall I found portraits of the women and children. Above them the words, "Be careful of them; they are our women and children."'

'And the women and children?'

'Nobody saw them come out.'

'What do you mean?'

'Gone.' The fool shows his palms. 'All disappeared.'

'But how can four hundred women and children disappear?'

'That is the very question I asked my good friends over there. How can four hundred women and children simply disappear? That man there – the fat one who carries white mice in his pack and dribbles in his sleep – he laughed when I asked him and from his pocket he took out a woman's finger with a gold ring on it. So perhaps only the bodies of the women and children disappeared, but their fingers somehow remained.'

When I wake in the night the garden is silent. For a moment I fear that the men have moved on without me but then in the moonlight I see their bulky shadows beneath the rifles. What I also see, moving quickly among them, is the unmistakable figure of the fool. Tiptoeing from figure to sleeping figure, the fool stops, stoops, then seems to whisper something into the ear of each man. As he leans down, the men stir. Some raise their heads a little, some seem to whisper back, but all settle when the fool has spoken to them. My heart is lifted by this act of love and I fall contentedly back to sleep.

When I wake again at dawn the fool is gone. I try to

rouse the men, but they will not be roused, sleeping, as they do, on pillows of their own blood.

And so the dream ends, although dreams do not end, they retreat into a point in our minds where we may occasionally revisit them.

I thought of the fool, envying his strength, as I climbed another ladder. This one was sturdy and sound and I had no fear that it was going to break when it bore my weight. I arrived through the wearisomely familiar trap into another room, circled it once, as had become my habit, and approached the next ladder, my arms like a sleepwalker's, already stiffly outstretched in anticipation. But, because I was now so attuned to the tower (particularly to its climate), I stopped dead when I felt a fresh breeze in my hair. Had I imagined it? I stepped forward and stood directly beneath the trapdoor and felt the breeze full on my upturned face. Perhaps, finally, my climb had been rewarded and I was coming to the top of the tower. I clambered up greedily and this time did not pause at the next room, for the breeze was stronger. Another floor and it was stronger still. It could have been imagination but I also sensed moisture in the air, glorious rain perhaps. One more climb and now there was no doubt in my mind that the top of the tower was just above me. The breeze had become a wind. There was, indeed, moisture in it; I could also discern a light from above me, more bright than that which had penetrated the tower through the mean windows. A further floor, one more, and then I was out into the air and standing gratefully on a circular terrace, open to the elements. There was a flagpole at the centre of the terrace (I had emerged just beside it) and, set against the low crenellated wall, a solid wooden chair – the throne, perhaps, of the flag-raiser. The wind was strong, I felt it pushing me back and I was grateful for the security offered by the wall which surrounded the tower. I anchored my arm around the flagpole and looked around me. As I have already suggested, the wall was low which seemed to indicate that the crenellations were decorative. And if, indeed, this was the case then the implication was that the tower I had climbed was a folly and had no function, military or otherwise (for a while I had believed it to be a lighthouse). Did it, therefore, have no purpose at all beyond the amusement it had afforded the man who commissioned it? My pride would not allow this. If I had climbed a folly, wasted a day of labour, then I was the fool. And surely a folly was a temporary thing, a whim, not built to endure. No man in his right mind would commission a folly of such a height with walls of such width.

I was, of course, consumed by curiosity over what I would see from the vantage point of the enormous height of the tower. Standing at the flagpole, at the centre of the circle of the terrace, I could see nothing around me but the grey of the sky. I released my hold on the flagpole and approached the wall. Because the wind continued to push me away I dropped to my knees and proceeded by crawling. Taking hold of the cold stone wall, I peered down the sheer face of the tower. I was marooned in a sea of cold cloud and could see nothing beneath it. I made my way to the flag-raiser's throne and sat, contemplating my predicament.

The tower had cheated me. It had promised an answer and stranded me without a destination. I had been more than a day without food or water. I had no option but to climb back down and apply myself to the trapdoor. No option but one: if I threw myself from the tower would I die? It seemed likely, if not inevitable.

And then, from the sky above me, I heard a whine. I looked up, and close by I saw a small, silver aeroplane. It passed slowly and sailed away through the clouds.

I contemplated its passing for only a moment before standing and returning to the trapdoor. Kneeling beside it I peered down into the well of the tower. Before my resolve failed me completely I turned, my feet found the rungs below and I climbed down into the first chamber.

Without pausing at each level, my descent of the tower was achieved in half the time it had taken me to climb. As I continued, the temperature rose and eventually the clouds, which had obscured the view from the small windows, melted away and once again I saw sunlight. When, finally, I arrived at the chamber above the shop it came as no surprise to me that the trapdoor which had dropped shut, imprisoning me, was now open. I did not dwell in the living quarters of the shop but descended the stairs, emerged through the beaded curtain and arrived behind the counter where I found the woman waiting patiently for custom.

She turned, startled, as she heard the beads of the curtain fall.

I walked quickly past her and out into the sunlight where I drew in great breaths of air before retreating to the sanctuary of the shelter on the promenade where I remained, watching the people of the town pass me by.

3

If one arrives at a railway station for the first time and then, on the following day, one passes that same station, the traveller's mature self deprecates the innocence he felt on his arrival. A single night in a new destination is sufficient for one to achieve such maturity. First impressions of a place rarely linger once the streets have become familiar. Complicated junctions, unfamiliar alleys, become allies once one has passed along them twice and savoured the satisfaction of recognition. A new arrival in a place can therefore achieve as great a sense of belonging as one who has lived in the town all his life. Rudeness or indifference towards the stranger do not dent this sense of belonging, only his humour.

My experiences in the tower had tainted my expectations. I had been in but not of the town, present but not part. I carried this contradiction with me when I rose from my bench and set off along the promenade. Having encountered only two people prior to my climb – the doctor and the woman from the shop – and having spent a day in isolation, I found the pace of the people who paraded towards and away from me rather frantic. A woman in black garb pushing a pram ahead of me was soon several hundred yards away. A boy cycling towards me was past and gone almost as soon as I had registered his approach. Two gentlemen who stood and chatted idly, hands in pockets, beside a public house, seemed to be jabbering at each other in a language I could not recognise. When I passed them, the nearest gent turned his besuited back towards me. I imagined he was expecting me to demand money from him, but nothing was further from the truth. I did, however, crave some human warmth. A handshake would have sufficed, even a smile, but my experiences with the shop woman had made me cautious of approaching another callous stranger.

With the two jabbering gentlemen behind me and listening now to the harsh call of the gulls high above me, I chose to divert from the promenade along a narrow street of white cottages. The street was devoid of people. As I walked inland the town's character began to impress itself upon me. Passing any judgment on a town by the sea is impossible until one can find a place within that town where the sea is not visible. I have been to places where the hold of the sea is such that, even at the furthest point inland, you are aware of it, as though the salt has been used in the mortar of the buildings. In other places, once the sea is out of sight it is forgotten, the architecture of the buildings remedying the deficiency of a proper fourth town boundary. I suspect that the origination of the place dictates its subsequent attitude. A fishing port will continue to pay its dues to the sea whereas a village sited on a clifftop may perhaps feel no reference need be made. The cottages on the narrow street seemed to belong to the sea and I was grateful. At the end of the row, I emerged into a wide, busy thoroughfare. Immediately ahead of me there was a large grey-faced building. One of the two wide doors at the top of the stone steps was open and seemed to be bidding me inside.

In the small hallway was an umbrella stand which held a single umbrella. The air in the hall was a salty mix of the old and the new (here the currents met and mingled). There were then two inner doors with patterned smoked-glass panels, neither of which was locked. I paused, caught in a momentary indecision as to which door to enter through, and elected to choose the one to the right (confounding an observer who would, I feel, have expected me to enter through the left-hand door). The door swung easily inwards on long brass hinges and I proceeded into the first room, which proved to be a tall vault of wooden display cases, all labelled, and in which, at the centre, there stood a wide square table bearing a large model of the town. I had, it seemed, stumbled across the town's museum. The ceiling of the room was high and vaulted and there were skylights in it. The floor was wooden (it was a light wood) and waxed to a high polish. The room, like the interior of most municipal buildings, was overheated, the heat rising through polished brass grilles in the floor. Beneath these grilles ran gulleys of pipes. The glass cases, stacked several feet high, contained stuffed birds of many species and colours in vignettes representative of their natural habitat. But it was the model of the town that took my attention. The floor creaked as I crossed it and would have drawn attention to me had I not been alone in the room.

I was soon party to the view of the town that I had been cheated of at the summit of the tower. Indeed, I sensed that the model-maker had been obliged to acknowledge this for he had attached gauze representations of clouds around the tower itself which, of course, dominated the vista. The buildings of the town were arranged around this landmark in semicircles which radiated inland like ripples cast by the tower itself. Various thoroughfares cut straight through these semicircles like the sun's rays. I took up a new position on the far side of the table and saw now that from above the impression of the town was that of a halved wheel, the tower being the axle. The boundary of the town was unblemished, the outermost semicircle of buildings representing the furthest extent of the development. Beyond that boundary, the model-maker had rendered the fields and hedges and trees with a care equivalent to

that which he had employed on the buildings. A single road
meandered inland across these fields and terminated at the
table's edge (a little to my right-hand side). It twisted several
times for no apparent reason of gradient or natural obstacle,
which led one towards the belief that few of the townsfolk ever felt the need to leave the place in any urgency. I
reached out and touched a ploughed field with my moist
fingertips. It seemed that the model had been made of
some hard plaster compound. It was cold and rough to the
touch and a little of the paint came away on my fingers.
As I examined the residue I heard a cough to the rear of
me. When I turned I saw a man standing at an open gallery
which ran high across the far wall of the building. His
fingers were laced together and he was watching me with
a keen interest. He did not call out, nor did he remon-
strate, but I was immediately aware by his proprietorial
stance that this was the museum keeper. The man was
elderly and dressed in black; his jacket was slightly too small
for him and his stomach made the buttons strain. He was
wearing a peaked cap and brightly polished boots. His face
held the immobility of those who spend their days in the
silent custodianship of artefacts. His eyes, however, were
those of a child. Individuals who choose to toil in such
mausoleums tend to be those who find a great companionship with the dead of any species.

When one meets the gaze of another it is rare to find

no acknowledgment in the eyes, if not in the muscles surrounding them, or even in the musculature of the entire face. I nodded hospitably and smiled (voluntarily, therefore unfelt, but none the less symbolic of welcome) but the museum keeper's expression did not change and I was left to infer a disapproval that had not necessarily been expressed. I maintained my smile which was now reconstituted to express apology for touching the model; a slight terseness around the mouth indicating some displeasure – although the displeasure was, of course, directed towards my own behaviour. I held it as I turned away from the man. In doing this I did not allow him the satisfaction of winning the exchange between us. But I felt his presence at my back for the subsequent minutes I spent at the table. If I had left the room at this point then he would have triumphed. My only hope at salvaging some pride was to reach out and touch the model once more. But I was not bold enough. Neither of us made any movement for a period of two or three minutes, and I suspect I felt the agony of this more than he. Finally I could bear it no longer. I briskly left the table and went to stand beside the display cases full of stuffed birds, breathing freely once again.

The exhibits did not captivate me although I marvelled at the taxidermist's art. In one case a blue bird stood on a snowy twig and peered into a mirrored stream. There was another at the water's edge; each stared at the other's reflection. The snow glistened (some crystal had been employed to achieve the effect). None of the birds was in flight although in one display a tawny owl was frozen with its wings outstretched as if it had been startled. It was while I was looking at the owl that I heard the museum keeper's footsteps proceeding slowly along the gallery behind me; when the noise ceased and I turned once more he was gone. A door at the end of the gallery stood open. I watched the dark rectangle for a moment, but, convinced I was now alone and once more unobserved, I left the birds and returned to the model. My curiosity over the layout of the town itself was satisfied and only now did I look along the seashore in an attempt to discern my point of arrival. And there, some distance along the beach, I saw a tiny figure prostrate upon the sand.

Why this alarmed me so much I do not know but I hurried from the room towards the nearest door. When I was through it I knew that this was not the one I had used to enter the museum. There were two stairways behind it, one which led up towards the gallery, another down into the basement. Because I had no desire to encounter the keeper I took the stairs to the basement and, once through the door, entered another vault of display cases. These were larger than those in the room above; none was smaller than three feet high, and most were six or seven feet. They were set out in a corridor

45

with a distance of five or six feet between them. Behind each row, therefore, was a tall vacant space some thirty feet wide. Either the cases had been moved out from the walls for some purpose of redecoration, or the visitor was expected to gain something from the experience of walking along the confined corridor (although one inevitably approached it in some trepidation). And none could have been unmoved by what they contained: an honour guard of grisly human figures, all standing dutifully in a dignified fashion, all dressed in formal attire, but all with a deathly pallor and the flesh in some decay. Some, and I must assume they were the older specimens, had almost no skin at all bar a few strips which clung to the bones like dry leather. An elderly couple in rotting marriage attire stood arm in arm in a vile parody of their wedding day. A child in a good grey suit with a black velvet collar peered out of his case with a troubled expression. His hands were clasped behind his back as if he was expecting, or receiving, some perpetual admonishment. The case beside him was empty but the bottom was sanded like that of a caged bird.

The air in the room was thick, the light was low, each case having its own internal source of illumination. I felt no macabre compulsion to stand and stare at these figures. They neither drew me to them nor repelled me, and surely one or the other was the intent. I left the museum by the front door and was careful to walk away without being seen to hurry.

Society is a net of fish swung fresh from the sea. We twist together in the enforced proximity of the net, but some of us fall out and lie thrashing on the deck until we expire. Such has been my lot since I left the army and the companionship of the fool (each day I expect him to reappear — quite suddenly, at my shoulder, or approaching me along some dark alley). The notion returned to me as I rejoined the main thoroughfare of the town. It had begun to rain and people were hurrying along the street wearing the looks of indignation that rain promotes. Watching them, I felt again a strong desire for companionship, a desire which was unexpectedly gratified when first my left arm and then my right was seized and I felt myself being forcibly marched along the street at a pace that I was quite unprepared for. It therefore took some moments for my indignation to arrive, the shock of the enforced march almost literally having taken my breath away.

4

'What is this!' I mustered, though all this outburst provoked
was a laugh from the fellow at my right. He was a stocky,
muscular ruffian of the type who makes a tidy but precarious living from his brawn. His head was shaved of hair,
he had a red, slightly bulbous nose on which the pores were
large and deep, and deep-set, exhausted eyes. I have known
many such men. They are never content, feeling, as they
do, that the better world intended for them lies just beyond
their reach. Each of my abductors was wearing a long coat
made of the skins of small animals, sewn together with
little art. The fellow at my left was quite a different type.
Unlike his swarthy co-conspirator who smelled quite dank,
this one wore scent. His face was delicate. He had a high
forehead and an auburn tint to his long, swept-back hair.
He was tall and graceful and I felt that there was no strength
at all in the grip he was using on my arm.

Once more I asked the fellows to release me, which of
course had no effect. And before I could ask a third time
I found myself manhandled through a low doorway and
down a single stone step into the smoky, dark den of a

coffee house. The stocky fellow led me to a booth and shoved me in, positioning himself on the bench next to me. The dandy, meanwhile, made his way to the woman at the counter and what he said to her provoked her into pouring thick brown liquid into three large cups which the fellow then brought over to the booth. After sliding onto the bench at the far side of the table, he looked at me for a moment, blinked, and the act of blinking eradicated the rather hostile expression from his face. When he thrust his hand towards me across the table he was smiling quite charmingly.

It took me some time in the fellows' company to make myself understood by them, and vice versa. I render the conversations as I remember them without the lengthy asides, the hand signals, the furrowed brows, employed as we struggled to find a common currency.

The graceful fellow's name seemed to be Pinch. (I say 'seemed'; what I mean is that this was the only approximation he was happy to subscribe to.) The other's was Oliver McDuke although Pinch called him Duke and so, therefore, did I. The relationship between them was odd. Not, as I had first imagined, that of master and servant, but neither was it on an equal footing. Duke seemed a little in awe of Pinch and listened intently when he spoke. When it was Duke's turn, Pinch listened equally intently although with a fond, knowing encouragement, provoking further observations by agreeing wholeheartedly with whatever he had to say. Brawn and brain awarded equal respect to the other. I felt myself in the company of two fellows who had only recently found themselves brought together; when they exchanged looks it was with an unveiled delight as if neither could imagine their luck at having found the other. Indeed, if there was a deficiency in either of them, then the other more than made up for it.

After some preamble, Pinch explained that the coffee we were drinking was 'robustas', which he preferred.

'From the Congo,' Duke added, handling it as if it were a bright new fact which had recently been coined and brought to his attention. ('Frum dur Conger' is what he actually said.) Pinch concurred, in the manner of the proud begetter of that fact. He gestured grandly towards a brown, unframed map on the wall beside the counter. It was too dark to make out any of the details but I took it to be a map of the Congo.

The rain continued to fall heavily on the street outside. When another man came in through the low door a stream preceded him down the stone step and made a miniature lake by the counter. The opening of the door caused a bell to ring and when it did all of the white faces in the room were turned in concert towards the new arrival.

Pinch and Duke fell silent, both taking further sips of coffee. Occasionally Pinch smiled at me in a reassuring fashion. Unsure as to what part I was expected to play, I remained silent. Duke filled his pipe from a leather pouch and lit it. When he blew blue billows of smoke towards me I smelled the farmyard.

Pinch, having completed his deliberations, made it known to me that they had first seen me from their boat. They had been fishing and Duke had spotted me on the shore, although he had believed what he had seen to be a corpse. When I signalled an understanding of this, Duke nodded heavily, remembering the moment. They had watched me for a while, and it seems that when I stood, Duke was not only surprised, but also a little dismayed. I suspect he would have preferred it if I had remained a corpse on the shore. Through Duke's telescope they had then watched me walking towards the town, but had been concerned when I reached the doctor's house and paused to look in his window. I suggested that this had been solely out of curiosity but Pinch seemed unconvinced. I justified it by suggesting that I had not meant any harm, which provoked a short exchange between the two men, the content of which eluded me. I had, it seems, not only woken the doctor; my singing had also alarmed the woman in the shop.

By now I was sure that Pinch and Duke were officials, employed in some capacity within the town. Were they asking me to leave? Or had I broken some law and was in the process of being arrested? I could draw little from the manner of Pinch and Duke. In listing my misdemeanours, they did so without any censure. In fact, from the tone of their voices, the catalogue of my actions could have been simply that – two men, having observed another, merely sharing the fruits of their observations for the single purpose of passing some time. If Duke had not been blocking my exit from the booth I would at this moment have attempted to walk away. But he continued to draw on his pipe while Pinch stared at me in a not unfriendly fashion across the table.

After another eternity of silence, I tried to ascertain the nature of my crime but Pinch would not be drawn. All he would offer was that the two men considered me a kindred spirit and wanted to warn me that I was in some kind of danger. From what or whom, they would or could not say. I assured them that all I wished was to remain in the town for a while, and then go on my way.

Pinch and Duke looked at each other again and then Duke asked what my intention had been in choosing to visit the town.

'I have no purpose,' I tried to explain. 'Not yet. Although a purpose will become evident. I'm sure of it.'

In turn, Pinch questioned what I would do if no such purpose presented itself. I answered that I would move on. He then quizzed me further on my motive for remaining, the essence of which seemed to be whether the *only* reason

I would leave the town would be because I could find no reason to stay. I had no choice, having given the matter some consideration, but to agree that this would indeed be the case.

Finally, I was asked how, when the time came, I would leave the town. To which I replied that I would take the road that led inland. 'And if the road inland is closed?' Pinch asked. 'Then I'll go by boat,' I said. Duke then warned me not to attempt to steal their boat, should I be tempted, and I told him that I had never stolen anything in my life. Duke nodded his head in reply and a moment later I was alone in the booth, the door to the street swinging shut and the rain continuing to fall.

I finished my coffee at leisure, taking some time now to look around me at the inhabitants of the other booths. They were all men and most were sitting alone. Almost all of them were smoking pipes; their ropes of blue smoke were tethered to the cloud that hung over the room. I could almost sense their busy thoughts and soon fell into my own sombre reflections about my childhood.

When I was a child I would awake at dawn to the thunderous bells of the cathedral. In my haste I would dress clumsily, all the time watching my mother sleeping in the single bed beside mine. She was the rock at the centre of my life. I always believed my love for her was greater than that which I felt for God (which I knew was wrong). It was certainly a more profound love than that which I felt for the priests. My mother slept soundly but, asleep or awake, she was never at peace. I was pained by the strain I saw in my mother's face. Her tightly closed eyes gave the impression that, were she not holding them shut, they would spring open and she would be robbed of a valuable hour of sleep. She treasured her sleep, hoarding it to ward off the trials of the day.

I would kiss my mother's forehead and linger over her to brush the thin hair from her face. She would roll away from me and mutter crossly. But she was not cross with me and therefore I did not fear her anger. She was never angry with me, although often angry at those who taunted me. I would then run downstairs and out into the embrace of the sleeping town. Glancing up once towards the iron-balconied third-floor apartment where my mother slept, I would run off, my arms outstretched like wings.

On that day, I remember, my habitual eagerness to join the world was even greater than usual. In the afternoon of the previous day, I had watched the rebels rise and swarm and take the town almost without a shot. I saw men I knew bearing cumbersome ancient weapons. They shepherded other men who were also familiar to me into doorways, down alleys, into the backs of trucks. I called and waved when I spied a friend. None returned my wave except for the young apprentice stonemason who, on seeing me, clowned and shrugged and doffed his dusty cap until a blow from the stock of a rifle stilled his smile and sent him sprawling to the ground. I ran towards him but a soldier held me gently back.

'Where are you taking my friend?' I asked him.

'To a place he'll be happier,' the man said.

'Will I see him again?'

'One day,' he replied, and I believed him because I never questioned the wisdom of adults.

I then joined the crowds following the red and gold standard to the cathedral. In the distance I heard the military trumpets proclaiming a state of war. The brass merged discordantly with the cathedral bells. When I reached the cathedral and walked through the huge doors into the beauty and cold, the people were singing a *Salve Regina*.

By the evening the town had been transformed. The guards who had been quick to join the rebellion stood on street corners, alert with a new sense of purpose. Officers tested their authority by barking orders.

A wintry heaviness had arrived with the rising, driving out the summer peace of my ancient city. The people I had known and relied upon were now cautious of any existing friendship or alliance. I walked to the fish market but the women who were washing down the slabs had no time for me. None laughed when I picked up a black eel and draped it round my shoulders like a scarf. When I removed it I felt my face burn. Even my friend the priest, who had always received me politely (if occasionally wearily), pretended not to hear me when I called from across the street. It was through this betrayal more than any other that I learned how serious were the events that had overtaken my beloved city.

My character, I now understand, had been formed by regular beatings. I came to accept that such punishments were as important a part of my life as the all-encompassing love of my mother. The pain inflicted upon me by other children was to be endured. Pain was the penance I paid for the goodness I found in adults. The more scars I took to them, the more love I earned.

My dawn wanderings had no pattern and no clear plan. I followed the golden paths laid down for me by the rays of the rising sun, trying always to dodge the shadows by turning into the streets which would maintain the sun full on my face. As I came into the wide thoroughfare I immediately saw a figure sprawled in the shadows: a man, face down, his legs splayed. As a child I enjoyed waking drunks. Sometimes they would pay me for this service. Occasionally they would curse me, but, having woken, they would always rise and stagger away towards their beds. There was, however, something about the man's stance that put me immediately on my guard. I looked across towards the City Hall to see whether there were any early risers who could help me. Although the door was open nobody was passing through it. I gathered my courage and approached the body. It was very still. I nudged a leg with my toe. It gave a little but it felt full and heavy like a sack of corn. I leaned down and looked into the man's eyes, which were open but seemed as dead as those of the fish in the market. I reached out and gently touched the man's face.

It was cold.

I knelt down, closed my eyes and prayed. I opened one eye and saw that my prayer had not been answered. I prayed harder but it had no effect, although I heard a shout which I thought my prayers might have provoked. A stout man was hurrying towards me, clasping his jacket shut with his right hand while his left fanned the air behind him as if it was propelling him along. I immediately recognised one of my friends: an important man called Ruis, one of the Commissioners of Justice. Ruis, who had no children of his own, enjoyed fussing over me. He delivered a gift to me every birthday, but it was always left with my mother after I had retired to bed. I was strictly advised that Ruis required no thanks. My mother reserved for him an awe she granted to few outside the Church.

When Ruis reached me, he stood trying to catch his breath. His face was grey and tired.

'I think the man is dead,' I told him.

Ruis peered down and said, 'Yes, my boy, I think he is.'

'What shall we do?'

The Commissioner, removing his hat and handing it to me, took my elbow for support and knelt on creaking limbs. He straightened the man's arms and legs. The tidied corpse, robbed of its mime of death, grew in dignity.

'Shall we pray?' I asked him.

'I saw you praying. I have to make a report now.'

'Can I help you?'

'No. No. It's something I must do alone, child. Hurry away. It doesn't do to linger around the dead.'

Ruis waited for me to leave but I was reluctant. I had never seen a body before.

'Yesterday . . .' I began.

'Yes?'

'Some boys said they wanted to fight.'

Wearily, the Commissioner replied, 'Boys always want to be heroes.'

'They asked me to go with them.'

The Commissioner stood and put his arm around my shoulders. 'It takes more than a scarlet beret to become a soldier,' he said.

'I know. To be a soldier you must be brave.'

'But, more importantly, you must understand what you are fighting for.'

'I do understand.'

'Do you understand what it means to kill?'

'Yes.'

The Commissioner, having led me away from the corpse, steered me round to face it. At that moment the sun crept above the apartments and lit the body, throwing a wide shadow behind it. 'That is what it means to kill. Could you do that to a man with whom you had no quarrel?'

'I'm not afraid,' I told him.

The Commissioner looked at me and I know that he understood. For in that corpse I saw a premonition of my own death. Behind us the sun had risen to light the steeples of the cathedral. At that moment they looked like golden ladders leaning against the wall of the sky.

When I left the coffee shop in the late morning I saw Pinch and Duke watching me from an alley. When they saw I had seen them they fell into conversation as if that was what they had been engaged in all along. Duke now had a dog with him on a short rope. The animal, some kind of mastiff, was strong-shouldered and panted heavily from the mere exertion of standing still. I fancied that the two of them, man and beast, were in some way related.

When I rounded a corner I lingered in a doorway for a while and soon enough Pinch and Duke walked past, some distance behind the leashed mastiff. I stood in the shadows, and although the high sun searched for me, it failed to find me. Shortly afterwards I set off in the other direction. By now, the rain having continued to fall, the gutters of the streets ran full with winty rivers of grey. A rainbow framed the town.

Having seen the road inland on the town model, it seemed prudent at this point to seek it out. If it did become necessary to leave the place in some haste I thought it wise to have planned the means of escape. In my mind I had a clear memory of the layout of the streets and knew that a right turn awaited me a short distance ahead. Meanwhile, I studied the shops that I passed. Few exhibited their wares in the windows and none carried a sign; it was only by peering inside that one could ascertain the nature of the shop's trade. In the recesses of the first I saw loaves of bread on floured wooden trays. In the next, bright yellow wheels of cheese. In another, a counter, above which ran a silver rail from which various feathered fowl were suspended by their trussed red claws. My hunger, which had abated, returned, but I had no money, nor did I have anything to sell; from the charity I had thus far received I thought it unlikely any of the shopkeepers would hand over their goods without immediate payment.

Away from the temptation of the shops again, I found myself in a poorer street. The dwellings were tall and dense and the roofs seemed to lean towards each other like drunks in conversation. Clothes were strung to dry between the higher storeys. Children played about the puddles of the street; a broken street barrow served as an island which a boy defended from the mob, a wooden stick for a sword. I watched the battle progress as he parried an attack with quick thrusts. But when they saw me a shout went up and they ran away in fear, scattering their sticks on the cobbles. A shutter slammed open against a wall above me and a woman looked down. Women have a sharp sense for danger. Her breasts were white and full above her blouse. She saw a stranger and she deduced a threat. Her face withdrew. When I heard a dog bark I was fearful that Pinch and Duke had discovered me, but the dog was nowhere to be seen. I then found myself drenched by a quick cascade of filthy water as the woman above me emptied a bucket on my head. I heard the laughter of children echo from the houses and immediately small sharp faces appeared like rats in the doorways and windows. I roared with anger and their noses were withdrawn. I extended my arms like wings and I flew, or at least I attempted to give the impression of a huge bird in flight, as I set off at quite a pace down the street. When I reached the end of it I halted and slowly lowered my arms, curious to see the effect I had made on the woman and children. I sensed a crowd behind me and sure enough, when I did turn, cautiously as I regained my breath and with some ceremony, across the street was strung a chain of townsfolk. They had emerged quickly from their dark dens. Children stood in the spaces between them. There were two waistcoated men among them, both of whom looked menacing and tough. One swung a chain. Nine or ten women stood shoulder to shoulder. The younger ones were handsome, the older ones were not. There seemed to be twin sisters who wore identical striped dresses and looked cruelly towards me. The older women wore a more naked menace. Children milled close to them within the shadows of their protection.

I called to them, 'I mean you no harm!' (as if a single stranger could do harm to such a mob!). The broader man, whom I assumed to be the leader, showed his teeth which were brown and broken and looked like the oiled cogs of a machine. He swung his chain like a whip and struck sparks from the street. A child came forward and for a moment I thought the hand of friendship was to be extended towards me. But the lad had made a cake of filth from the mud on the street and threw it at my face. Emboldened, the others came towards me, the line holding, each keeping a similar distance between himself and the next.

Pinch's warning came back to me and I now regretted slipping away from them. To save myself from a beating I should have run but I was paralysed by fear. My legs felt leaden, as if the labour of the climb up the tower and the lack of sustenance had been dropped like a great weight on to my shoulders. The chain swung again. A woman called a threat. The children continued their approach. I did not turn to run, instead I waited, curious now as to what fate awaited me.

When the children reached me they did not immediately strike out. They left it to the adults to abuse me in an attempt to provoke an anger which would then justify their violence. But they spoke so loudly, so quickly and with such hatred that my untutored ear could not translate the insults they were making. I tried to understand them, but I expect I looked like a fool. In the absence of a threat, ignorance (or its idiot son, stupidity) is regrettably considered equally worthy of punishment. And that I imagine was the justification which brought the two men and the women towards me.

5

When I came to the rain had stopped. At first, I assumed myself still to be on the street where I had fallen. My mind had not spared me the details of the incident although I had no notion of the time that had passed since then. Wherever I had been taken I was no longer in the echoing street. I heard birdsong. There was no other sound except that of flowing water – a river or a stream somewhere in the distance? And was I lying on the ground? No. This had become a game now, a game I allowed myself to play as a reward for the pain I was enduring. No sight, just the sound and the feel of the ground below me. I reached out in anticipation of earth or pebbles. But my right hand encountered nothing, simply a wide expanse of air. Very well, what of my left? What would that find? Was it wood? Yes. A plank? Yes. Several planks? The deck of a ship? Cautiously I opened my eyes and I saw the sky above me. It was not still. I moved below it and the clouds' gentle parade proceeded above me. How cheerful and new is the world when one has feared that one may never see it again.

I deduced that I was in a cart progressing at walking pace along a track which was not in a town. In fact I sensed that we (whoever we were) were well away from the town. I had a picture of the model in my head and as my mind served it to me I saw a tiny representation of the cart travelling along the winding road away from the tower and towards the boundary of the model. But how far had we come, and who was driving the horse? The more I considered my escape, the more grateful I felt. I attempted to sit up and look around me.

But I could not sit up. Although my arms were free my neck was bound to the planks of the cart. I reached out and discovered that my waist and my legs were similarly secured. Whether or not this was for my own good, to prevent me from rolling from the wagon, I could not guess. I made a rapid inspection of the thick ropes which bound me and concluded that without a knife I would be unlikely to free myself. All I could therefore do was engage whoever was driving the cart in conversation, and I resolved to do this as gently as I could. It came to me that perhaps I had been given up for dead and was being taken away from the town to be disposed of. This would explain why my body had been secured while my arms remained free. With this possibility in mind I examined my feelings. To have the experience of consciousness while dead is, I imagine, rare. Few have reported on it although curiosity has provoked many to attempt to communicate with those beyond the grave. If death is what many promise it to be then how would I know?

I would surely know by speaking out loud. If I spoke and the cart driver answered then I was surely alive. If he did not then, although it did not necessarily mean that I had passed away, the possibility of it would not yet have been removed.

To speak, then. But what to say? The confidence that had been granted to me when meeting Pinch and Duke was now gone and I was left feeling much as I had done when I first encountered the woman in the tower. Duke had suggested my singing had alarmed her, but I imagined that if I was in the position of the man or woman driving the cart, I would have been grateful for a gentle song even if it emanated from a man whom I had previously considered a corpse. So I sang. It was a song the fool had taught me, a lilting air which began slowly but built in strength as the story progressed. It concerned two brothers, fishermen like their father, who, late one night, took their father's boat and set out to sea. The following day was their father's birthday and, being poor, neither of the young men could afford to buy him a gift. They considered that a good catch would bring the old man pleasure. Not only could he sell it, but it would also enable him to rest for a day without the need to leave the harbour to earn his keep.

This being a song sung by the fool, tragedy soon struck. Just before dawn, a storm blew up, the boat capsized and the brothers were thrown overboard. As it does in many sea villages, superstition in this place held that fishermen should never be taught to swim. The fates would therefore not be tempted to test how well they fared in the water.

The following morning, when their father woke, he knew immediately that his sons were gone. He dressed and, without waking his wife, ran to the shore to search for them. There he found his boat washed up, undamaged, almost as if he had run it gently aground. The sail was up and the new sun was drying it. He clambered aboard, stood at the stern and looked out towards the sun. Not so very far away he saw a figure in the water swimming strongly towards the shore. He shielded his eyes and peered harder.

At this point, for three verses, the song breaks from the story of the fisherman and his sons and calls upon the listener to consider how much of our lives we spend in anticipation and examines the various forms this anticipation takes. When we return to the fisherman, the figure in the water is close enough for him to see. It is, in fact, not one man but two – the swimmer has a man on his back. They are, of course, the two brothers, who stumble finally from the sea. The swimmer, the older brother, collapses in exhaustion. The younger one lifts him, carries him and lays him at his father's feet. An explanation is offered at this point as to why the older brother is unburdened by superstition and why (to the alarm of his father) he had learned to swim. His mother taught him as a child. She had not been born into the fishing community and therefore did not consider herself bound by its codes.

And so the older brother wakes, the three men cling to each other, the brothers confess that they have no gift for their father's birthday, their father tells them they have come back alive and that is the greatest gift they could have presented to him. The brothers return home to sleep. Their mother stirs as they enter the house. The song ends with the older son berating her for tempting the fates by teaching him to swim. 'But it saved your life,' his mother tells him. 'Rather, it nearly cost us our lives,' the son replies.

A song concerning fate and superstition seemed appropriate to the journey I was taking and it did not entirely surprise me that it did not immediately provoke comment from the cart driver. But time went on, an interval far longer than one would have required to ruminate over the debate between the son and his mother. A few birds sailed over me, flying away in the direction from which we had come. The clouds continued to go by. The sky remained grey. The track was even and our progress was gentle. Finally I was inclined to cast caution aside and appeal directly to the driver: 'Who are you and where are you taking me?' This garnered no response beyond the steady clip-clopping of the horse's hoofs on the lane. And listening to them it struck me that I had heard no rein or whip, no word nor breath nor oath. Perhaps there was no driver. Perhaps the carthorse knew the journey so well he did not need to be steered. And as the idea entered my mind I became certain that this was the case.

Momentarily, this calmed me and assuaged my fear. But as the journey progressed I became unsettled. Like the cart, it seemed that I was now at the mercy of fate. I began to see that since I had arrived on the beach I had had little influence over my destiny. I had merely been following some predetermined route which was now leading towards the next destination.

6

I slept, although I do not know for how long. When I awoke I was sure that we were approaching our destination. The ringing of the hoofs on the stones of the lane was now provoking echoes from a distant wall; the sound of the cart's approach soon came crowding back towards it. I saw a plume of brown woodsmoke above me and then the outer wall of a building reaching up towards the sky. The stone was grey and had been hewn in large rectangular blocks. Rows of arched windows latticed in black indicated that the building was three storeys high. Above it, I could see a number of ornate chimney pots on which birds perched and looked down on me.

Without pausing for a gate to be opened we proceeded through an archway (the stone of it was green with damp) and came out into the fresh light of a courtyard where the horse drew to a halt. It took one step forward and made some adjustments to its stance before it seemed content to rest and snuffle and wait patiently to be attended to. I took comfort from it and tried to calm myself as I too waited for release from my shackles. The clink of the bridle, the small shifts in the cart's position, the movement of the clouds above me across the wide sky were the only distractions. I heard no voices from the building nor any evidence of industry, but I sensed that I was not alone.

A door finally opened a short distance from my left-hand side. No bolt was drawn but a catch was lifted. Footsteps approached across stone; a single set, ripe with the bluster of purpose. They paused beyond my sight. I was aware that I was being looked at (weighed up, measured, judged; some adjudication was being made, some mental ledger completed). The footsteps then continued, a cluck or a click was voiced and the horse stepped on. I watched what I could see of the windows in the wall above me as I was borne along. And then we were again in another brief noisy tunnel of shadow as we proceeded through a further archway. The courtyard beyond this was darker and smaller; an area of stables and workshops and kitchens, perhaps. The walls that surrounded me here were unbroken by windows and devoid of any ornament although ivy clung to the damp brick. I fancied the sun did not choose to visit this place.

When we drew to a halt there was a brief pause before the buckles were undone and the horse released from the harness binding it to the cart. With some sadness I heard it being led away into a stall which was closed behind it. I waited to be removed from my own shackles. Instead, the footsteps retreated through the archway.

At this moment my fear took a turn towards anger. I had, so far as I knew, committed no crime, and yet I had been brought to this place without any consideration of my own preferences. My fingers returned to the ropes which bound me at the waist. Perhaps the movement of the cart had had some effect, perhaps I had not previously examined them fully, but I found that I was not, as I had believed, bound tightly. With some effort I got the rope undone and with further efforts also freed my neck. I sat up and looked around me. The horse peered at me from its stall; its gaze was unwavering, reproachful but not devoid of humour. It seemed to be in accord with my own feelings. 'How dare they bring you here against your will!' it seemed to be suggesting.

I dropped down to the ground and steadied myself on my feet. My legs felt hollow, as though the blood had ceased to circulate. I slapped them like unruly children and they regained their weight and substance. The place was cold. It was late afternoon and my coat was damp. The larger courtyard promised more warmth so I walked beneath the archway towards the main house. I did not, however, stride immediately across to the door and hammer upon it as I felt that I had every right to do. Instead, I waited beneath the protection of the shadow of the wall. The courtyard was neat and square and utterly empty. An orderly mind oversaw this dwelling. There was no sound from the building and I did not feel drawn to approach it. The ungated archway in the far wall beckoned; my freedom lay beyond it. But I was held by the magnetism of curiosity.

I have long believed that life offers a series of riddles to its purpose. Fate, or destiny, draws us in one direction but it is only the current in which we swim. We are always at liberty to strike out towards the bank of the river and climb out. I once saw a crusader on a tomb. He slept in stone, his hands clasped across his chest. I was with the fool and the fool asked me what purpose I could discern for that crusader. I answered that for the fool the crusader's purpose was to provoke the question he had just posed. For me, the purpose was to reply. We each make our own charts of the world, navigate our own shallows and perils. Each question we pose and every answer we give is a further stage on a journey towards a greater understanding. That the crusader came to me again as I waited in the courtyard I took to be an indication that I should not yet choose freedom, but must first discover the reason for my capture.

I retreated to the smaller courtyard, reasoning that I would find an alternative entrance to the house through the servants' quarters. The horse watched me pass and seemed to be in accord with the decision I had made. He momentarily put aside his own ruminations to will this agreement towards me. I nodded towards him in thanks for the journey and he, after a pause of some moments, nodded back. I suspected that I had offended him, that he felt we had reached such a level of understanding that it made thanks superfluous. It is rarely recognised as such, but once a certain level of intimacy has been reached, gratitude can be seen as an insult. Thanks are most often used to salve the conscience of the offerer. As with praise, the recipient has no pocket in which to keep them.

Beside the stables was a large door. It was locked. I peered in through a small opening in the wall and saw that the arched brick chamber housed a black funeral carriage. I have always found that such carriages have a peculiar life of their own, as if they are in some way animate objects. As I stared in and saw the rats busy beneath the carriage, the large spiders in the silver hammocks above it and the small birds which patrolled around it, I heard a wood-saw rasping from a doorway in the furthest corner of the court-yard. When the rasping ceased, wood fell with a round clatter to the floor. The sawing then continued. Reasoning that a man at his labours is less likely to threaten a stranger, I approached the open door.

I stood at the threshold looking into a dim room which appeared to be a mix of workshop and kitchen. The man, who was now planing a length of wood, sending off blossoms of fragrant shavings to the floor, paused to run his thumb along the planed length merely to enjoy the pleasure of its smoothness. He wore a long leather apron, a white collarless shirt and trousers of rough, heavy tweed. To his task he gave a large part of himself which, I imagined, he would or could not make available in any other regard. He was, in short, a craftsman. He turned to face me only when he had completed his planing of the wood and stood ankle deep in the drift of shavings. Behind him a table was laden with food (meats and breads and some cheeses). Eight unmatched chairs stood away from the table at such angles as to suggest the diners had scattered in haste. A fire glowed in the aperture of a large metal range. Several candles had burned out on the table, others clung to life. An oil lantern was hung above the craftsman's head.

The man, who was younger than I had believed when I first saw him, seemed put out at having been distracted from his labours and not in the least curious at my presence. His face was that of a tin soldier: naïve and open. He discerned that the reason I stood at the door was because of the food on the table behind him and waved for me to enter, to sit at the table and to partake in it. Returning to his task, he set his plank of planed wood against others which rested against the wall.

I hurried to the table. My hunger, which had remained dormant for almost two days, was reawakened when the odour of the meats and the cheeses assailed my nostrils. I felt a stranger to myself as I hacked ham from the bone, put the edge of the knife to my lips and fell upon the salted flesh which melted immediately in my mouth. But in my impatience I could not wait for the flesh to dissolve, could not enjoy the flavour and texture of the meat, did not pause as it provoked a hot, sudden thirst in me; my hunger was greater. Like an animal I tore with my teeth at a round loaf of stale bread and felt the serrations to my tender mouth, but the yellow butter which I spread upon it salved the pain. Soon the first bite of soft warm cheese (which waited to flow across the table, so ripe was it) cloyed the salt of my saliva, its strength sending tiny flames of pleasure up against the roof of my mouth. I poured a glass of warm beer from the stone jug and gulped it down in one. More cheese, more bread. At the centre of the table was the carcass of a roasted chicken. The breast meat was gone, leaving a hollow skeleton which danced in the flickering candle flame. A leg, however, remained unscathed. I tore it away and felt only a small resistance as it broke with a clip from the socket and shed jelly across the table. My teeth met bone as they ground down through the soft white meat. Each subsequent bite took notice of the last, navigating the most efficient route around the flesh. And slowly, as my hunger retreated, I began to take pleasure from the feast so that the next time I returned to the cheese I laid it on a piece of the buttered bread, and then took a spoonful of thick brown pickle which I spread upon it. When this concoction was embraced by my jaws it was the flavour of

77

the pickle which declared itself first: a mush of vinegar and salt and sugar, and then the fresh wonder of apples bursting through it all like a sunrise; another mouthful of cheese and then bread and butter and I was finally sated.

Shamed, I found the courage to look again at the craftsman, hoping that he had been so engrossed in his work that he had not witnessed my gluttony. He stood at the open door, leaning against the jamb, looking out at the courtyard and smoking a pipe. Because he was not currently regarding me and I was unaware of the moment at which he had lit his pipe, we could each of us happily pretend that the gluttony had not taken place. I coughed to indicate that I had finished and stood, pushing the chair away from the table with a scrape as the feet rasped against the crude stone of the floor. But the man did not seem in the least bit interested in me. Granted, he paid me the brief courtesy of a glance, but he then turned away and applied himself again to his pipe. A woman, I have no doubt, would have found his character to be a challenge to her patience. I had been in his presence for a very little time but already I knew that he would not be rushed, that he considered any physical task worthy of great attention, and that he regarded himself the single best judge of what warranted his attention. I knew that, like a farmer whose livelihood makes greater claims on him than can any human tie, the craftsman would pay little heed to any man except his employer, and only then under sufferance. I left him to his labours without a further word; I was ill-tempered without good reason.

The door beside the table seemed the most obvious way to find access to the house — which was where I hoped I would find the answers I was seeking, the reason for my captivity.

The corridor beyond the door was long and unlit. No windows gave on to it, so I could only guide myself by the small illumination of daylight which came from the far end and found a way in beneath some of the poorer-fitting doors. The floor was stone. Several pairs of riding boots stood against the wall, toes out. I passed a number of closed doors but, unlike those in the tower, I felt no compulsion to open them. There was a power within this place much greater than I. Not simply the power of wealth (I have held my own in many conversations with rich men), but something more. If I liken it to the threat one feels when waking at night from some nightmare perhaps you will understand what I mean; even those who choose not to believe in a deity cannot deny that they have woken and sensed a fear of something unknown. If evil is real and is the threat we feel at night, then surely so is good.

The corridor twisted to the right. Along it now at shoulder height there ran a number of lengths of cord in which tension was maintained by weights and brass wheels. The cords went through a high aperture into one of the rooms. I paused to examine them and as I did I heard a creak from the far end of the corridor, the cord tightened, one of the brass wheels turned a little way and a bell was heard ringing on a spring within the room. Immediately, the door opened and a girl came out, tidying her hair and removing an apron. Without breaking her stride, she hung it on a hook beside the door. She gave me no second glance as she hurried away to answer the call of the bell.

Because she had left the door of her sanctuary ajar, I felt that permission was not required for me to go inside. She had been alone here at her single chair against a small table, sitting beside a tidy fire and a blacked stove (cold), and reading a book by the light of a window. The window gave out on to the smaller courtyard. Looking out, I could see directly across to the room in which I had eaten, and could even see the craftsman still at his labours. The horse was no longer gazing from its stall, but I took pleasure from the sight of a place that was familiar to me.

It was by looking at the girl's book, which lay open on the table, that I finally knew I was in a place I did not belong. I recognised none of the words on the page although the letters were all familiar. Nor could I guess the meaning. I attempted to speak the words out loud, but they meant nothing to me, they were guttural and unpleasant to the ear. The girl came in as I returned the book to the table. She started at the sight of me; she was a child so conditioned to deference that she immediately assumed that I occupied a higher station in life. She curtseyed and averted her eyes, a little flustered. But then, as her eyes slowly returned to me, and saw my torn and filthy clothes, my unshaven, wounded face, I could see a moment of wonder in her. Perhaps, for the first time, she found herself in the presence of a man who warranted no more respect than a dog. But she could not trust this instinct. Not yet.

She spoke to me. Although I could make no sense of them I imagined they were words of harsh interrogation. I shrugged and gestured in apology and told her that I did not understand. That she did not then understand me sufficed to get the message across to her. I sensed that she did not want me to leave, and I did not want to leave, yet we had no business with each other. The girl determined to find herself a purpose, and it was evident that the purpose, or service, she could most easily provide was to do something about improving my appearance. To this end she walked around me, and when she was at my back I felt her sharp fingers clutch a handful of the cloth of my coat and feel its dampness and roughness. When she faced me again she gestured that I should remove my coat and hand it to her. She seemed surprised at the weight of the cloth, but she laid the coat across her arm and I understood that

I must follow her as she went out into the corridor, turning right, and going back in the direction from which I had come.

Several doors later, she opened one and went into a room in which there were a number of tubs and kettles, a raging fire, a range, and a floor which was awash with water and suds. She peered into one of the tubs and dropped in my coat. Taking a wooden paddle, she pushed the cloth beneath the surface. We both watched it submerge beneath the white with some curiosity. Next, I was invited to remove my breeches, and, indeed, the rest of my clothes. The girl turned away and handed me a linen sheet which I wound around myself to save us both embarrassment. My breeches, shirt, braces and other pieces went the same way as the jacket and were also prodded beneath the soapy surface. With both hands she hefted a heavy kettle on to the stove and unhooked a large tub from the wall. While the kettle waited to boil she filled pitchers with water and began to fill up the big tub. I made an offer to help but the girl preferred to work alone. When she had poured the streaming, streaming water from the kettle into the tub, she stood beside it and waited for me to remove my sheet and climb in. My nakedness was to be her reward. She was no longer coy but stood quite brazenly waiting for me to reveal myself to her. This I did and she looked at me with some curiosity as I grasped the sides of the tub and lowered myself in.

Thankfully she did not offer to soap me. Instead she set about agitating the clothes in the other tub while I soaked. It was a great pleasure feeling the warmth of the water caressing my body, teasing away the pains of the beating, lulling me towards a sleep I could not resist.

When I awoke, it was dusk. The water in the tub was quite cold. The fire had burned out and the girl was gone. When I looked into the other tub I saw that she had taken my clothes with her — and also removed the sheet from the room.

7

I have never been ashamed of my naked body. It is, after all, to protect the sensibilities of others and not ourselves that we have learned to shroud our nakedness. We make many such assumptions in life, and so ingrained are they within us that we choose not to question any of them. It was practical concern, however, that weighed heavy on my mind as I searched frantically for something to cover myself. I was shivering with the cold. My skin had shrunk and was wrinkled. My fingers were numb and white, the prints raised up into crevices as deep as thumbnails. The washroom, however, was devoid of anything I could use for such a purpose. A prisoner once more, I resigned myself to a night of torture as the chill spread through my body. So used was I to the assumption of imprisonment that it was a good many minutes before I even went to the door and tested the latch. Immediately it lifted. The girl, then, had left me to rest and had perhaps taken my clothes elsewhere to dry them. I could only assume that she had been delayed in her return.

I heard lowered voices from the corridor and waited just

inside the door for whoever it was to pass. One of the men sounded quite infirm and was breathing heavily. I anticipated an elderly gentleman going by. Instead, I saw that the panting was emanating from Duke's mastiff who was tugging his leash taut as he led the way towards the main part of the house. Pinch and Duke followed shortly behind him. Their arms were linked together and they were engaged in a lively but whispered dialogue. The mastiff paused by my door and raised its ugly head, but Duke tugged him on, and the threat of a beating was a greater incentive to him than satisfying his curiosity.

After they had gone – the stench of the dog, or Duke, lingering – I waited for a moment to see whether anybody followed, but the corridor was silent. Looking once to the right and once to the left, I stole along to the room where I had first encountered the servant girl. Without pausing to knock, I opened the door of her sanctuary and went in. Looking up from her book, she seemed in the candlelight not in the least surprised to see me. My clothes were laid across a flat rack which was attached to ropes and pulleys and had been hoisted high above our heads into the warm air that collected at the ceiling (the stove was now lit). The child immediately went to the clasp where the rope had been tied, loosened the rope, and the rack, swinging a little, was lowered. She held it, maintaining the tension, as I took the clothes and dressed myself.

My body welcomed the warmth and softness of the cloth like a new skin. Previously it had resisted and squirmed beneath the salt and filth. How had she dried them so quickly? I can only assume the creel beside the fire held the reason. The girl tugged at the cord and the empty rack was raised again, swinging towards the ceiling. When it was sufficiently high, she tied it off. At this point we regarded each other. She was unchanged; she wore the clothes I had seen her dressed in before. But she saw me anew and was obliged to reconsider what she thought of me. That I owed her something for her kindness was unspoken between us. But the question she was asking herself was how much further that obligation went. Were we equals? Was she now expected to serve me? Or should she raise an alarm? She returned to her chair and I could not read the decision she had made. At the very least, by the fact that she had not run into the corridor screaming, I assumed that she saw me as a threat neither to herself nor to the household at large. And I imagined that perhaps she was looking for some distraction from her chores. Further deliberations were curtailed by the ringing of one of the bells on the board above her head. At the sound of it she stood. Her face lost the softness and curiosity I had seen on it when I entered the room, and she was now a servant girl once more: nothing more, and nothing less. Dumb with anticipation, devoid of any judgment about the task she was to be presented with, she left the room and our time together was gone. I had no choice but to follow her out, and I watched and listened as first her shape disappeared and then the sound of her footsteps was swallowed by the silence of the long dark corridor.

I searched the burdened silence but could hear nothing and so I went along the corridor. After a short while I heard a laugh and, a little further on, the sound of accompanying voices. A violin was being played. This was not a fiddler engaged to lift the spirits and make the feet tap, but a musician of some culture engaged in a dialogue with the minds of those who were listening. A cultured gathering, then, which led me to consider more carefully how I should approach the room.

By the time I reached the tall double doors I had come to no decision. Behind them was contained the party and the violinist; there was also a strong, clear voice pitched at such a level that it seemed to be demanding attention. The hubbub below it was, however, loud enough to suggest that there were as many as a hundred or so people in the room. The clear voice of reason spoke and paused, spoke and paused, and then there was the sound of a gavel on a wooden block. After that, some applause was offered before the voice again paused.

I pushed open the doors and was confronted immediately by the vastness of the room. I had assumed it to be of a scale in keeping with the corridor and the washroom, but the ceiling was high, the walls on each side as wide apart as hedges in a field, the far wall within sight but a hundred paces away from me. The space was made to seem even larger by the mirrors that lined both side walls, creating an infinity of reflections of the men who stood about and smoked and talked; of the women who sat at the tables; of the children who ran and played around them. I should estimate there were close on two hundred people in the room and, presiding over them, an imposing gent on a raised dais at the far end. He sat behind a table which was stacked with papers, a gavel in his right hand, and a pewter dish at the centre. As I entered, a boy came to the dais, climbed the three steps to the table, took away the dish and replaced it with another bearing a short length of candle. The man lit the wick, then called the room to order; there was a quietening of the conversation as a number of the men and women in the room bowed their heads towards the papers they held in their hands. Some discussion followed, before the auctioneer offered a tentative figure towards the audience and a hand was, after a short pause, raised.

I was now five or six steps into the room, and concerned that the opened doors behind me might call attention to my presence there. I had not been conscious of any interest since I entered, although so overwhelmed had I been by

89

the room that I might have been unaware of any stir I might have caused. But when I turned to close the doors, I found that they were already shut; a man inclined his head towards me, acknowledging that he had taken the task upon himself and had been glad to do so. I inclined my head towards him in thanks. His gaze, however, lingered on me a little too long for politeness, and the uneasiness I had felt on entering the house returned. I saw a steadiness in his gaze, and questioned myself about the circumstances under which I would find myself staring in such a way. I concluded this: that I would have been party to some information concerning the fate of the fellow and, for a brief moment, had witnessed the effect on him of encountering this fate. The man must have been aware of my interest in him, for at this point he folded his arms and made a great show of looking around the room, moving his head up and down, left and right, as if he was searching for somebody. But he remained by the doors, blocking my exit. And he was strong. I could see that his shoulders were wide and his chest broad. Some cowardice in me prevented me from approaching the fellow and asking him to shift aside. If I had been proved right, and had been prevented from leaving the room, then I would have found myself once more imprisoned. By choosing not to, I therefore renounced the role that may have been assigned to me and, for the time being at least, remained a free man.

A crowd can embrace a stranger or it can turn its back. Whichever stance it adopts is dictated by the stranger's attitude. If one approaches, head bowed, with the expectation of being rebuffed, then one will be rebuffed. Advance with a smile and a hand outstretched and one will be met with the same enthusiasm. (There are other aspects to this. If one whispers to a friend, a friend will whisper back. We are only the echoes.) In the city which was made of wood (where the buglers sailed out of the clocktower) I soon found an acceptance among the crowd in the square although I knew that there was some distance I was obliged to travel before that general kinship turned to camaraderie. In truth, when I left that city I had failed to find such camaraderie. When a drunk man is sober he may regret the optimism he was granted by the wine. That is how I felt when I left the city; a chance for belonging had passed me by and I regret it to this day.

But we learn from our mistakes, and that we do is our only salvation, which is why I found a welcoming face to wear as I approached the small group that stood in a circle close by the door. This comprised two young women; an elderly man with a rosy face who smiled but was clearly quite deaf, his smile an attempt to radiate to those around him an understanding of and agreement with the conversation; and three fellows of similar age. The stoutest of the three wore a velvet jacket, was ruddy-faced, quite drunk, and held an empty glass in his hand. The other two men and the two young women were paying court to this fellow, allowing him to speak without interruption. The looks that were passed between the women held some restrained amusement at the stout fellow's expense. That the two other young fellows could not share in this amusement I took to mean that the stout fellow was in some way superior to them, but lived outside the companionship of women. The women would not have risked such exchanges if he had a wife of his own, or if a woman who belonged to him stood sentry at his shoulder.

The stout fellow saw me first, which is how it was destined to be. He was the gatekeeper to my acceptance here. And when he saw me he paused in his conversation, which alerted the others to turn round and face me. At this point I felt obliged to remove my hat and bow in greeting. This was not to indicate deference, but merely some universal token of greeting. I could not have shaken hands with all in the group; it would have seemed as though I was passing a hat around the circle to collect not their money but their approval. Nevertheless, the bow marked me out as being foreign to those in the room which, I knew, granted them the power to adjudicate how seriously I should be taken. They waited for the stout fellow to make this adjudication and I could see that he was dallying. He put his head back a little way and fixed his eye on me, to indicate to the other fellows that he intended to test me out before he was prepared to include me. He spoke, but so quickly that I had no clue as to the nature of the question he was putting to me. After he had spoken he looked towards the fellows for approval, which was granted. As I had done with the servant girl, I answered that I did not understand, and the fact that he did not understand what I said to him conveyed the message I had intended. This made the fellow uncertain. He could not intimidate me with his words; I had no doubt by now that that was what he intended. So how could he maintain his position of influence?

The answer is that he could not. The power was immediately wrested from him by one of the women. She had a lively, pretty face and clearly enjoyed the stout fellow's discomfort. Perhaps she had been waiting for the moment when she could make her voice heard within the group, but after a sharp enquiry to one of the two young fellows, who nodded, she faced me and spoke quite slowly. Although, from the expression on her face, I could glean some understanding (a polite question, I think, about my place of origin), I was no wiser than I had been when the stout fellow questioned me. I smiled at her but shrugged my shoulders. This was a sorry defeat for the woman who had staked much by claiming the responsibility of becoming my interpreter. Her good grace vanished and the others seemed to feel the need to come to her defence. They looked towards me as though the entire fault for the lack of understanding between us lay with me.

I had no choice but to bow again and back a step away from them as I did so. I knew that as I turned and walked away the stout fellow would see fit to comment, that this comment would provoke some easily bought laughter, and the good humour of the group would thus be restored. This indeed proved to be the case. I heard the laughter, most shrill from the woman, as I forged a way through the other groups and gatherings, having no wish now to join any of them. I was looking for Pinch and Duke. For although I had no particular desire to renew our acquaintance, at least with them there lay the possibility of some communication between us. But Pinch and Duke were nowhere to be found. Soon I was standing close to the dais at the edge of the tide of folk. A hush fell and the voice of reason spoke.

I had been aware of the man because he sat on the dais, and I could therefore see his body and head above the crowd. What stood beside him I had not yet glimpsed, but it was a large oak chest. Various other pieces of furniture were about the room behind him: the contents, perhaps, of a large house being sold off. There seemed to be a good deal of interest in the chest because the dialogue between the man on the dais and the people throughout the room continued for many minutes. Finally, there were only two bidding, a woman and a man, and the bids went between them until the man shook his head and the woman, with delight, clapped her hands together and was congratulatd by the people within her group. I could see all of this because the woman stood directly to the side of me and I had been aware of her growing interest in me as the auction continued.

A boy came and took from her a piece of paper. She stroked the boy's cheek as he left and took the paper to the man at the dais. In turn, he folded it and placed it upon a pile of other such pieces of paper which, because all of the pieces had been folded, looked set to fall. But the auction was over. The man secured a narrow red ribbon around the folded papers, put them under his arm, and left the dais. He then walked away to the far end of the room and exited it through a door which was opened for him by a servant as he approached it. Such was the man's importance. The woman who had bought the chest now went to it and raised its lid and looked inside. The chest was ornate and carved and was, so far as I could see, empty. The woman, however, continued to peer inside it. None of the others had joined her in her inspection which led me to wonder why this was so, but the woman seemed content. She was examining it for her own purposes, not for the approval of the others.

I heard a voice and when I turned around Pinch and Duke were behind me. It was, of course, Pinch who had spoken. I was grateful to have found them but could not tell how they felt on seeing me. Duke was watching me closely, although what he was anticipating I could not guess. He seemed filthier than he had been when last we met, as though he had been employed digging in some field. Pinch reminded me that I had been warned, although about what he chose not to share. I explained to him that I had been struck on the head, tied to a cart and brought here.

Pinch turned to Duke and repeated, 'He was tied to a cart and brought here.' Duke, it seemed, now required my statements to be interpreted before understanding them.

Pinch asked when the attack had taken place. The question met with Duke's approval because he leaned forward a little, waiting for my reply.

'It was . . . it was today, or yesterday.'

'Ha!' Duke said.

I suggested that I was not entirely sure whether I was now a prisoner, or merely a guest. Pinch looked at Duke in delight. They shook hands as if they were sealing a bet, leading me to understand that this had been the subject of some previous discussion between the two of them. I could see the woman who had bought the chest watching us. She lowered the lid and approached; Pinch and Duke melted away from her presence. She regarded me as she had regarded the boy who had taken the paper from her and she stroked my cheek.

'Why are you so sad?' she seemed to ask me.

I heard her quite well and I understood her equally, but I could not comprehend why she had spoken to me in such a way. I heard a gale of laughter from behind me and turned to see that it had emanated from Pinch and Duke, although they immediately struck poses to suggest that they were not listening. The woman appeared not to have heard them. I did not answer her question because I could not, but she reached out and took my hand.

8

'Would you sing for me?' the woman seemed to ask. And so sweetly did she ask it, I had no choice but to comply with her request.

Holding me by the hand, she led me to the dais where I climbed the three steps to stand facing the crowd. Slowly silence came over the room as first one group, then another, saw that I was waiting to perform. Pinch and Duke were nowhere to be seen although the echo of their presence was strong. I chose to sing a song I had learned from my mother. She had a beautiful voice, though she never aired it in public, indeed she seemed almost ashamed of her gift. But she would sing to me as she bathed me, encouraging me to join in, sheltering my frail voice beneath hers, never hurrying or harrying, taking the strongest line herself and, when she knew that the time was right, leaving the tender silence for me to fill. I emerged from beneath her wing with a voice that had been tended by her; a fragile thing whose roots were strong. In the full sun of an audience it soon blossomed.

The song concerned a darker age and a man who tended

a field. Because there was little daylight in this world the crops were poor and the people were hungry. The man's only wealth lay in his pocket watch which his father had presented to him, and which he kept in his waistcoat. He had made a solemn promise to his father that the watch would never run down. But the man, in his anxiety to comply with his father's wishes, overwound it soon after his father died. He could not afford to repair the piece, and that he felt it tight against his ribs all day as he worked he considered an appropriate reminder and punishment for his foolhardiness. But when the crops failed and his children screamed from hunger, he found a greater suffering than guilt. Indeed, he soon found himself blaming his father for his predicament. After all, had he not inherited the poor fields from him then he could have travelled and established himself in a better place.

One morning, after another fitful night broken by the cries of his children and the admonishments of his wife, he fled the house, went out to the fields and crushed the pocket watch under his heel into the earth. The glass broke and so fine was the case that it too disintegrated under the weight of his boot. And then, rather than returning home, the man spent the following week in an inn where he drank at the expense of others and became increasingly wretched.

Seven days later, sober and fearful, he returned home. The route he took passed his fields, and as he approached he saw a number of folk standing in a line at the edge, their attention caught by something within the boundaries. He ran ahead, afraid that some dreadful fate had befallen one of his children, but when he reached the cordon of folk, he saw a golden crop of wheat almost three feet high. The crop extended throughout his fields, and had begun to spread beyond to those who owned the land around his. More remarkable than this, however, was that above the golden fields the sun shone quite brightly. He had never seen the sun so bright, so conditioned had he become to the half-light of his terrible world.

The man knew that the crop had come from his father's pocket watch. He had sown seeds of golden time and the wheat was the result. He was gratified but he faced a dilemma: if he harvested the crop, would it return the following year? And if he did cut it down, would the sun no longer shine?

He tried to explain this to his wife, but she would hear nothing of it. The children were so hungry he had no choice but to bring in the harvest. Therefore, on the following day, he took out his scythe, and within a few days the harvest was in. The sun continued to shine for a while, but gradually the days grew shorter, the rains came, the air grew cold, winter set in and darkness once more prevailed.

The man, however, had been shrewd. He had kept enough back from his harvest to sow the seeds for a new season and, the following year, after the frosts were gone, he sowed his new crop. Again it grew, bringing not only fresh golden wheat, but also the bright sun. And the dark land was no longer dark, for the man had sown the light back into the earth.

When the song ended, the people were silent. I would have liked to believe that I had enchanted them, but they stared with incomprehension. The woman, recognising this, led the applause (her hands held high at her chest, the claps loud and rapid), and she was regarded sufficiently well for her lead to be followed by the others. I climbed down from the dais and went to stand beside her. Once I was by her side none seemed inclined to approach her, and I could see that she was amused by this. Indeed, it was almost as if she had brought me to her to repel the folk who were in the room. Watch these people, she seemed to be telling me, see how you can learn from them, see how they fear you, but more that they fear themselves.

After she had tired of this game she took my hand and led me to the oak chest. She wanted to return to it as one often does when one has purchased a thing of beauty and searches anew for the clarity of that pleasure one felt at the first moment of ownership. She lifted the lid and we looked inside.

'It's quite empty, isn't it?' her expression seemed to

suggest, though it would have surprised me to have found anything in it. With a gesture, she invited me to accompany her as she made her exit from the room.

Leaving that place with the woman was a quite different experience from my arrival there. In her company I was accorded her status; as we walked through the room people paused in their conversations so that, should the woman have chosen to ask a question or make an observation, she would not have been required to interrupt them. We moved, therefore, carrying the silence with us. I think this amused the woman, and because it did, I assumed that such a state was novel to her. It was, of course, not novel to me. She held a smile upon her face. As we approached the tall doors they were opened for us, and when we had walked through they were closed behind us. At that point the woman's composure collapsed and she laughed out loud. I felt obliged to join her, although I could not share in her amusement for I did not understand its cause. Was she laughing because the people had been struck dumb by her choice of me as her new companion? Was she amused by their subservience? Was she amused by herself? Until I could discern the reason, I could not know how well I would like her. I had accompanied her from the room without protesting, therefore I had already accepted her terms, but if I was to play a part which required me to be more than a servant to her, I felt it important to judge her character.

It was to her credit that she immediately understood I was laughing for her and not for myself, and at that moment she stopped. Her amusement, however, remained — although, with a degree of slyness, it was now directed towards me.

I believe you're judging me, her look suggested. And in return I tried to explain that yes, I was, but it was for my own protection. I went on to explain that I had arrived in the town barely two days before, and told of the warnings I had received from Pinch and Duke . . . but when I mentioned their names she held up her hand to silence me. The world outside had come back to her and extinguished her smile, for which I was now sorry. But I was glad to have seen her intelligence used. I have always been attracted by it, for it protects the soul like the shell on a nut.

We walked then in our own silence which lay on us now like a cloth dampened and wrapped about our shoulders. This time she did not take my hand, and I of course could not have reached for hers. We passed along the corridor in a direction that led away from the kitchens, and by this route came eventually to a hallway and from there out into the courtyard where there were now many vehicles and men waiting and smoking. When she was seen an alert hush descended on the men. Those who were smoking took their pipes from their mouths as a mark of respect. Some bowed their heads. All looked from her to me; a judgment was being made as to whether she was accompanying me of her own free will. A powerfully built man then stepped forward, doffing his hat, and we followed him through the carriages to one that stood a little distance apart, closest to the gates. The man opened a door and offered his hand to the woman. She mounted the step without his assistance, the carriage cocked a little towards her, and then she was inside, the door firmly closed after her. The man climbed into the front and I waited for instruction, but the carriage pulled away and I stood in my stupidity watching it pass beneath the archway, sure that some opportunity had been missed.

Would I ever know my purpose here? I wondered. Would it be revealed to me, or must I choose one? I regretted losing the woman; at that moment I even regretted the loss of Pinch and Duke. But as I did, I heard the carriage draw to a halt beneath the archway. I hesitated, but then walked hastily towards it and, when I reached it, found that the door was open. The woman was looking straight ahead as if it was of no account to her whether I came inside or not. I forgave her for this, grateful that I had been offered another opportunity to share her company. I climbed in and took the seat facing hers. I pulled the door shut and we moved away. The springs were soft. We rocked from side to side as we travelled away from the place where I had bathed and met the servant girl and the craftsman. Night was falling and around us there was soon darkness. The woman instructed me to sit beside her, which I did. From politeness, I maintained some distance between us, but she pretended that I had taken offence at being abandoned in the courtyard and was punishing her by being cold towards her. I understood, then, the game we were to play and I moved close to her.

Her face was quite white in the light, her skin was clear. I looked closely at her proximate beauty; at her eyes, at her nose and her lips which were slightly parted over the pearls of her small teeth. I took her right hand which lay limply in her lap and brought it alive by caressing her palm. My thumb found a pulse at her wrist which beat more quickly as I laced her fingers around mine. I exerted some pressure on her hand and she returned it. I raised her hand to my lips and blew a soft breath upon it, then I took her fingers into my mouth and tasted them. Our faces were close now, and I could see a desire in her eyes, the hunger and delight which she had displayed when she lifted the lid of the chest. My own desire also grew, calling for the completion that her body would provide. But it is in taunting this urgency that our pleasure lies, and when I felt the woman's hands at my belt I gently guided them away. Only later did I succumb, for finally there is nothing the mind can do to preserve it from the demands of the body. We go away from ourselves in desire only to return when the journey is completed.

A question we must always ask is how much we have been changed by such journeys. I was changed, which is how I imagine one begins to understand what the poets call love.

But love, like happiness, takes many forms. Afterwards, I wanted to hold the woman to me, to feel her warm hair against my face, to smell her and to taste her, to make her a part of me so that I could be a part of her, but after lying for a while she pulled herself from her reverie and sat up sharply and pushed me away from her. I again took my position on the other seat, uncertain now as to my role. The woman adjusted her dress, and as her composure returned her good humour retreated. We completed the journey in silence. She would not meet my eye, and I was led by this to understand that what had passed between us must remain a secret. When the coach drew to a halt, she clambered across me to the door and rushed away. I waited for instruction in another courtyard, in another place I did not belong.

The driver came to the door and invited me to step out. A torch was alight and illuminated the face of the building, making it grand and stern. The man went to the horses and led them to the stables. I looked towards the building for some clue as to my purpose there. I thought I glimpsed the woman in a window above, but the figure moved away before I could be sure. Wearily I began to walk away; I had finally lost all hope of finding a place to belong. When I passed out of the courtyard and on to the road I looked around me at the landmarks bathed in the light of the moon. On the horizon, far to the east, I could see the tower and was reassured by it. I had no other destination in mind so I began to walk towards it. Immediately I heard a shout. I turned and saw the coachman waving to me to return. When I reached him, he led me through the main doorway of the house and into a large hallway. He then walked up the stairs and, a short distance along the corridor at the top, he pushed open the door to a bedchamber and I went inside. A candle was lit. There was a bed, a pitcher of water and a fire alight in the grate. Without removing my clothes I lay upon the bed and was immediately asleep.

9

Another morning greeted me, though for once I awoke on a bed, and in enjoying its comfort I was immediately reminded of my new circumstances. What had seemed dark and confusing on the previous night was by the light of the new day clean and clear. I rushed to the window and threw it open, wanting to feel the fresh breath of the day upon my face. I drew it deep inside, raising my face to the sun and closing my eyes so that the sensation of the warmth on my skin and the smell of the fields in my nostrils would not be bullied by the greed of my eyes for the sight of the world. And when I opened them I was not disappointed. Ahead and to the left and right were, indeed, fields, and they were a riot of colours. The colour, however, came not from what was planted there, but from yard upon yard of bright golden, red and orange fabrics which flew as standards from a thousand flagpoles. Fields of flags, fully raised, visible for as far as the eye could see. Each was unique, each patterned in squares. It was ludicrous, and yet it was not. When they were caught in the currents of the breeze it was apparent from which direction the wind blew and the changes it made from moment to moment. It was such a spectacle that I stood at the window for a long while enjoying it and making it my own. Nobody had a greater claim to the patterns drawn by the wind that morning than I, for I was (so far as I could judge) the sole witness. Whoever had planned this vision must surely have had this intention.

I wanted to share the moment, so grateful was I for it. And I regretted being alone, for unless I could share it, I was afraid I would be called a liar when I came to recall it. I turned in hope, but without expectation. There was, of course, nobody in the room. When I looked again at the fields, the sun had hidden itself behind a cloud and the standards glowed less brightly. I knew, however, that at that moment, I wanted the woman beside me. I was bold and hungry for her. I had waited too long for some role to be assigned to me and was now convinced that I must take one for myself. If she was the mistress of the house and the fields of flags, then I should be the master. I strode out into the corridor as if I had every right to demand the attention of every soul in that place. But the house was curiously silent. I waited but I could catch neither the echo of voices nor any sound of feet along the corridors. I peered down into the gloom and I could see that the place was wreathed in cobwebs. My feet made new marks in the dust on the floorboards. I looked above me and could see through a hole in the roof clear to the sky. A bird flew across my vision and settled beyond it. I stood and wondered and considered how long I had been here. Surely only a night had passed.

I was afraid that when I returned to the room in which I had slept the fields of flags would be gone, and of course they were. The comfortable bed in which I had slept was nothing more than a pile of sacking. I had woken too soon. The world had been prepared for somebody else and I had chanced upon their place in it. But everything was now back as it should be. I recalled at that moment that I had stirred in the night and heard a coach in the courtyard. Doubtless it had been the sound of the woman fleeing.

It seemed that I had been destined to live in a loveless world of dereliction and decay; that I would reach out for warmth only to find that the warmth did not endure. It had not always been thus, and I had to believe it would not always be thus, otherwise I might as well have lain back on that pile of sacks and waited for a more permanent sleep to overtake me.

What gave me the strength to walk out of that room was the woman and the feelings I still had for her. She was real. And she would not be far away. She had led me to the house and left me there, perhaps to rid herself of me. But I would not give up so easily.

I returned to the ground floor and was poised to leave

III

through the front doors when curiosity overtook me.
Perhaps a clue to the woman lay within those walls. I
wandered through the chill darkness and into a room where
the shutters were closed. A fine vertical line of daylight
marked the joins, and it was those which guided me over
so that I could pull up the black bolts. Illuminated, the
room proved to be an empty gallery where the marks of
the missing portraits were white rectangles, smoked with
dust at the edges. There were two empty plinths, and a
shattered marble bust on the floor. I wasted no more time
in there, having a sudden awareness that my life was being
consumed by that place and that I was worthy of more.

I made towards the door, but as I did so I heard laughter
from the rear of the house. So hungry was I for joy that
I ran towards it, my heart quickening. Out of the empty
gallery, along a corridor, through a room of broken statues,
into a scullery and out into a yard where I paused, waiting
and listening in the morning cold beside the red brick wall
of a kitchen garden. The wall was tall, but there was a gate
which was open some way along it. I approached it with
more caution, afraid that my presence would frighten off
whoever was beyond it. But when I heard laughter for a
second time, I discerned something old in it. It was as if
I had experienced a familiar taste, and one which was not
entirely welcome, for I felt my chest constrict and a fear
descend upon me. I paused, my back against the cold bricks

of the wall, trying to shed myself of it. I took two steps and stood at the open gate and was there confronted by the sight of a boy in a tree. He was smiling down at me. It seemed he had been anticipating me. He was a good distance from the ground, sitting on a thick bough. His feet were bare, his knees were skimmed, his face filthy.

I knew his sadness despite his smile because it was my own. I could not go to him and yet I felt that I must. He called out in a language I understood, 'Mother! See I've climbed the tree.'

From behind me, through me, around me, a woman walked and stood beneath the tree. Bruised by leaf shadows, she looked up towards her son. He dropped to the ground and stood beside her and she immediately gathered him to her and he buried his face in the fabric at her waist. I knew how those clothes smelled, I knew exactly how the boy felt: the warmth of the woman's body, the slight coarseness of her fingertips as they kneaded the tender skin of the boy's neck.

I had that day woken into another life. But the other life was also my own; a shutter had been opened and I had peered in. I found myself looking up through the tree towards the sun, and I no longer saw the child or the woman. But the memory had not saddened me. Instead it gave me strength. We walk the streets of our past many times in our life. As we grow old, some of us choose to linger there. And we must know them well, for until we do, we are destined to keep returning until we can find a way out.

10

I went from that place unconscious of the fact that I was walking. The rhythm of my footsteps lulled my mind into a state which was close to sleep. As a result I do not know what I was thinking as I walked. I was at rest and grateful for a while to have been freed from the torment of my thoughts. When I heard somebody whistling and found that it was me I returned to the day, refreshed. The sun had risen and sat high as my spirits. Birds sang in the hedges and played above the fields.

If I had been watching my progress across the model in the museum, I would have seen that I was approaching the town again, this time from the north-west, although I recall only one track having been represented on the model. The fields around me were ploughed, the soil dry and chalky. When I saw Pinch ahead of me, his muddy boot up on a stile, his left elbow upon his raised knee, his chin supported by his palm, perhaps I should have been surprised, but I was not. He was calling to Duke, who was out of my sight on the far side of a hedge. From the glee on Pinch's face, I could see that he was enjoying himself, but he did not go so far as to laugh out loud. He seemed to be restraining himself from allowing full rein to his pleasure.

I saw him give an almost imperceptible look in my direction. But, having glimpsed me, he chose not to acknowledge me. Because there was no hostility from him I continued my approach and was soon standing at his side, looking, as he did, across the stile and into the field. I could not immediately see Duke, although I could see the vile dog which was waiting some distance away, standing guard in the field beside a large root vegetable.

We stood in silence for a while, then Pinch suddenly called out a command whereupon two eyes magically appeared in the earthy face of the turnip. A mouth then opened below them to reveal teeth. It was only at that moment that I realised that what I had taken to be a vegetable was in fact Duke's head and that he had been buried up to the neck in the mud.

On another command from Pinch, Duke closed his eyes and then his mouth and was once more a vegetable. The purpose of this remained so far from my comprehension that I determined to waste no more of the day on it. While Pinch and Duke undoubtedly belonged to that town by the sea, it came to me that their logic was entirely their own, and not necessarily shared, or dictated, by the place they were in. There was a gentle malevolence about them, but it was not contagious because they had found in each other a suitable repository for it.

I left Pinch, sensing that he was disappointed that I had not engaged with him in a futile discussion concerning their activities. I did not even turn back when I heard the mastiff charging after me. And when it barked at my heels I did not break my stride. Soon it was behind me, and the further away from the field I went, the happier I became.

The tower stood on the horizon and served as a useful landmark for my destination. I could, of course, have walked away from the coast and the town, gone beyond the borders of the model, and started into another life, but I felt drawn back to that place. I determined that I would approach it this time not as a stranger and would perhaps find a better way to belong. I walked for an hour, enjoying the freedom and certainties of my body, and took some time to thank my maker for it. There is much simple pleasure to be had from the marvellous functioning of our limbs – they are finer than any machine. Our senses too, sentries to the world around us, are fine and wonderful companions. When I am alone, and when I remember, I spend time with each of them, exercising my sight and smell and touch. I therefore become more alert to the world around me.

After an hour, the tower a little higher on the horizon, I saw a red-faced, rotund fellow sitting at the side of the track. He looked exhausted, his knees drawn up to his chin.

In his right hand, which lay like something discarded beside him, he held the end of a length of thick rope. He saw me at the same moment that I saw him, raised his head a little way from the support of his knees, and stared towards me like a dog eliciting sympathy. I raised my hand in greeting but he did not raise his. He did, however, lift himself wearily to his feet, dust down his coat, pick up his tall hat and take up the tension in the rope. He looked along the line of it like a rifleman taking aim. When I reached him, he braced himself, digging his heels into the earth, and tugged at the rope. It did not budge so he applied his strength to it once more, again without result. I knew enough about the place by now to take this as an indication that I should join the fellow in his labours and therefore knelt down and picked up the end of the rope, which lay on the ground behind him. He took up his stance once again, looking back to ensure that I had done the same, and then we each applied ourself to the rope. Immediately it gave and a mark which had been made some way along it advanced towards us.

I should at this point explain that the rope went through a dense hedge and whatever it was connected to was invisible to us. The fellow, however, seemed gratified with the progress; he dashed to pick up a small stone which had lain at the previous position of the mark, and moved it to the new position. Rushing back to me he sat down and I sat beside him. He left the rope on the ground beside him as if he had no further interest in it, although by his glances towards it I knew that this indifference had been adopted for my benefit; as if, in my eyes, he would have been in some way diminished by his literal attachment to the rope. I did, however, learn something of him from the fact that he was prepared to release his hold on the rope – and this understanding heartened me and gave me strength. What I now knew was this: there was no man at the far end of the rope. My new companion would not have risked losing what he had won from the rope if he had feared that it would be tugged away from him. Instead, he would have tied it off or kept a firm hold on it.

I was, of course, curious to discover what the rope was attached to, and how long the fellow had been engaged in his endeavours, but I did not feel I could ask him outright. And if I sense a frustration in you that such a direct enquiry could not be made, you must trust me that in such a place no direct answer would have been forthcoming.

Having made progress with my assistance, the fellow seemed disinclined, at least for the time being, to exploit it further. His exhaustion gone, he seemed content to sit and wait and pass the time in my company. But within a very short period, the silence began to weigh heavily. Each time our eyes, which ranged around for entertainment, met, the enthusiasm diminished. Finally, I grew agitated and became impatient to return to the town, so I stood and, bowing my head in farewell to the fellow, walked away. Shortly afterwards a stone struck me on the back of my head. When I turned I saw the fellow looking towards me. Immediately he threw another stone and then another in my direction. Both of these fell harmlessly short. When he picked up another, my anger overwhelmed me to such an extent that, instead of running away, I ran towards him. He was strong, but so surprised, I think, by my approach that when I reached him and threw my fist at his face, he did not try to protect himself. His eyes blazed in alarm and his hand went to his full cheek which I had felt give a little when my fist connected. He turned away, cowering, his shoulder towards me, but I was intent on provoking him so I kicked him hard in the back with the heel of my boot. He slumped to the ground and whimpered, lying on his stomach, his fingers laced together over his neck. I raised my boot again but then saw myself for what I was. My anger was spent but it was good to have tasted it.

A thought came to my head as I walked away. Perhaps it came from the violence of the anger which had tightened the muscles of my neck, or perhaps from the memory of my childhood, but it was this: we are all murdered by our pasts. I examined it no further. Such thoughts rarely linger. Many crumble under scrutiny, and those that do not have often been borrowed. The thought was gone almost as soon as it arrived. The space it left was soon filled with guilt over the attack I had made on the fellow with the rope. I knew I would carry it with me for some time to come, unless I could assuage it. This I did by allowing myself to believe that it had been provoked by not one but three stones hurled in my direction. And if the second and third had fallen short, the first had not and could easily have injured me. When, some time later, I looked back towards the fellow, he was still sitting and contemplating the ground. The next time I looked he was out of sight.

A cloud appeared in the sky ahead of me, which I fancied looked like a fat man smoking a pipe. He was sitting cross-legged and wearing a fez. At that point my mind wandered away from me again, leaving me in that precious and precarious place where we can be at rest and free from torment.

At rest and free. At rest and free. At rest and free. My footsteps carried me on. My thoughts returned to my home.

II

Despite the protestations of Commissioner Ruis, from Burgos I travelled to Pamplona to join the army. I remember vividly how I was jostled as I waited in the barracks queue for my uniform. My hands were stained scarlet by the dye from the beret I was clutching. I passed the time by picturing myself in my new finery, marching swiftly up the Calle de Lain Carvo, drawing respectful looks from the men and admiring glances from the women. I saw myself calling up to my mother's balcony. On appearing, I imagined her holding her hand to her mouth in delight before dashing downstairs to crush me in an embrace that lasted until, breathless, I patted her back and begged her to release me.

The men in the queue behind me were scrapping good-naturedly in an effort to alleviate their boredom. We had been waiting for an hour, but for the past twenty minutes our progress along the cold, dim corridor had ceased entirely. I had become separated from the Burgos men shortly after the flag-festooned truck arrived in Pamplona, but I was comforting myself with thoughts of my mother; to bring her more closely to me I reached into my pocket for the scrap of cloth she had sprinkled with her scent and pushed into my hand as I was hauled up by my arms on to the flat-backed lorry to sit alongside the other volunteers.

The man standing immediately before me took three steps to close the gap that had opened up before him. He was contentedly reading a blue-bound book, resting his thick shoulder against the chalky wall. The man's hair was shorn to a bristle and I was fighting the urge to run my fingers over it, to test the sharpness of the stubble. At home I would not have given it a second thought.

'You.'

I felt myself being pushed in the small of my back. When the man reading the blue book turned to see who had been challenged, I smiled to win his support against the bully behind me. The smile was not returned. Dust fell from the wall as the reader resumed his position, now wary of me.

'You.'

I felt a more forceful shove in my back. I turned, cautious of a fist in my face, to confront my slovenly, open-mouthed tormentor. The man's tobacco-brown teeth were uneven and proceeded into the dark of his mouth like stepping stones into a sea cave.

'You stand behind us,' he ordered.

'But why?'

'Because we're hungry – and the sooner we get our uniforms the sooner we'll be fed.' The man nodded smugly. The others murmured assent.

'But,' I protested, 'I'm also hungry. I'm very hungry.' And I rubbed my stomach to indicate just how hungry I was.

'You're just a boy. Or so you tell us. You can wait. Stand behind us.' The man jacked a thumb over his shoulder.

Knowing it was useless to protest, I stood aside to allow the bully to take my place. The three men standing immediately behind him appeared to be part of the same group so, when they too had stepped forward, I attempted to take up a position in the queue after them. I was prevented from doing so by two men in bibbed overalls standing alertly side by side, who shuffled quickly forward, leaving no space for me in the line. The doleful, deferential expressions of the men masked a steely concern for their rights. Though I explained the situation to them, they shrugged and told me that their place was behind the group of three. This was the position they were allocated and this was the position they intended to maintain. The argument was borrowed by the handsome green-eyed boy who was standing alone next in the queue, although he suggested that if he was granted permission by somebody in authority he would gladly relinquish his place. He did, however, ask for this to be delivered in person.

I thanked the boy and walked on down the long line of

rugged but poor-looking working men. When a friendly face presented itself, I tentatively asked to join the queue, but nobody allowed me in. The most painful betrayal came from a man I recognised from home, an obsequious, pious man I had seen doff his cap to my mother on many Sunday mornings. One morning I had awoken to find him at the kitchen table, my mother giving him breakfast. When the man in the queue pretended not to know me, I was reminded of the day after the uprising and the way my world was changed by it. But the memory of home heartened me. It defined everything I knew, everything I was, from the cathedral lit by the fire of the searchlights at night to the tiny church of San Gil. Recalling these landmarks, I felt my fear diminishing and the tide of my happiness flooding back. By the time I reached the end of the line I was viewing my demotion in a positive light; I would, I now believed, have the choice of everything that was left on the quartermaster's shelves. Perhaps I would be given two uniforms in reward for my patience.

Where the queue ended, at a crucifix junction in the barracks' corridor, I stood on tiptoes to look out of a small arrow-slit window. I saw a fat military priest crossing the dusty parade ground, a heavy wooden cross bouncing high towards his throat with each step, and down again against the stiff khaki of his shirt. Three young *requetés* were being drilled by a squat, sweating man who barked out commands in a gravel voice. I watched them march and turn and turn smartly again under his relentless commands. A chevron of silver aeroplanes passed over the far rooftops, and when the sky was clear of them and the chalk lines of their trails had dissolved into the blue, the line ahead of me again began to move. But this time, rather than drawing swiftly to a halt again, the shuffling steps became a slow walk and I soon found myself passing the place in the corridor I had been ejected from a few minutes before.

I followed the tail of the crowd out into a large barrel-vaulted hall. When the queue broke from the constraints of the corridor the line spilled into a milling pool of men stretching their limbs, lighting cigarettes, laughing and slapping each other on the back as if they had endured a year of solitary confinement. I, too, was glad of the new space above me and the horizontal beams of sun through the high windows and the stale refectory smell of the hall. I was always content with progress, however slight. This was why, as a child, I walked and walked and was rarely still. What disappointed me was that there was no evidence of the uniforms. I had visualised long racks of pressed shirts, shelves of smart boots, tall wicker baskets with shiny belts and bright buckles spilling like snakes from the top. When I saw the green-eyed boy and asked him what he knew he shrugged and walked away. I stood at the edge of another group and posed the same question. Nobody chose to answer. I tried the two denim-clad men from the line. They dismissed me impatiently. I turned left and right and found other backs turned towards me. When a face did meet mine I could see no love or camaraderie in it.

The excitement of the journey from Burgos had faded, the enforced proximity of the men — first in the lorry, then in the corridor — was now gone and I was left wandering alone in a huge hall of strangers. I was hungry and I had no money. Worse, I had strayed too far from the sanctuary of my mother's apartment. I had never before been more than fifteen minutes from her side. I clutched the piece of perfumed cloth and rolled it between my thumb and second finger before touching the pinched fingers to my nose. The scent was fading.

I edged through the crowd of men to the wall. Requiring something solid at my back, I leaned against it and reached behind me for the cold reassurance of the stone. My heart slowed again. My world had a solid boundary to it — I could build more. The murmurs in the hall dimmed as a man climbed the steps to mount a dais at the window end of the room. I saw the yellow-tasselled beret, the lean open face, then the immaculately pressed khaki shirt of a young officer emerge through the plane of cigarette smoke to take the platform above the shoulders of the crowd. I felt an immediate affinity with the soldier as he looked round at the faces tilted expectantly towards him. Like my important friend, Ruis the Commissioner, he wore his authority with ease. By the time his slow searching glance had taken in the volunteers before him all of us felt as though the man had walked among us and shaken us firmly by the hand, perhaps even asked for a name and then solemnly repeated it to lodge it in his mind. Most striking, beyond the physical presence of the officer, was the patch sewn on to the left breast pocket of his shirt. Mounted on a square white lace cloth was a bleeding heart entwined with thorns.

The fellow welcomed us, his voice barely raised, prompting the volunteers to move closer to hear him continue, 'It is with regret I must inform you that there are – at this time – no more uniforms.' He waited, but nobody's disappointment was voiced. 'It is enough that you wear the scarlet beret with pride. There will be shirts and there will be equipment in days to come but none will be as important to you as the beret I see that most of you are carrying.' He left a moment for us to judge the significance before he moved briskly on to more practical matters: the winning of the war. 'In two days' time we depart for Madrid. Tomorrow you will return to this hall for instruction. Tonight, you may come here to eat. Until then I suggest you make the most of this time to consider the reasons that brought you to Pamplona. And if you are in any doubt, there will be – in one hour's time – a procession through the city led by the Archbishop of Toledo . . .'

The officer took a step back and rested his weight on the edge of a table. 'I counsel you now. This is not a war for the uncommitted. You may consider yourself fit for the rigours of battle – some of you may have experienced it before – but this is a fight for the soul of our country. And because we are fighting our countrymen, the enemy may not be easily identified. Every town along the enemy's line of retreat must be considered a battle zone. We have received orders today which serve to reinforce our belief that civil panic along the enemy's line of retreat will further demoralise them. Accidental destruction of enemy hospitals and ambulances has a highly demoralising effect on troops . . . And when we march triumphantly into Madrid – should we face any opposition – the streets will be put under immediate fire. There will be no distinction as to gender. The more ruthless we are, the more quickly shall we quell the hostile opposition and the more quickly will the restoration of Spain be effected.' The officer's attention lingered on the mute crowd. Only as he stepped down from the dais was the trance that had fallen over us broken and we cheered. The war had become real for us. Women were to be shot. The ambulances of the enemy were to be treated with the same hostility as their artillery. It was clearly a job for men with strong stomachs. Only one in the hall considered the task beyond him.

Commissioner Ruis had been right, early that morning

as he knelt beside the body of the man in the Burgos street. I could not know what it meant to kill in cold blood. But I had no time to dwell on my concerns as I was swept from the hall by the tide of men pressing towards the refectory doors, flooding the corridors, spilling down the steps towards the open streets to enjoy their last few hours of freedom before they joined the cause. I felt my legs lifted from the ground. My feet began to flail but I was trapped so tightly that I did not fall. Indeed, I did not touch the ground again until the volunteers emerged into the bright sunshine outside the barracks.

The men dispersed rapidly in groups of three or four, and, where new alliances had been formed, seven, eight or nine; a back-slapping carnival crowd hungry for food and thirsty for wine before they had to face the rigours of another day. But because the next day was to be like none before, so neither, they declared as they scurried from the barracks, should the celebrations be. Soon I was alone in the empty square. A child, holding his mother's hand, pointed towards me. The woman tried to pull the child away without allowing her gaze to meet mine, but the child was resolute. And he was strong.

'What is your name?' the boy said with pride in his voice; whatever name I offered to him it would not match the character of his own.

'My name?'

How long had it been since I had been challenged for my name?

'My name is Marcelino Merida,' I told the boy and I bowed to him and his mother took him away.

I reached into my pocket for my mother's piece of cloth. It was gone. My fingers scrabbled at the grit that lay along the pocket seam. I pinched at the minute stones and lifted them to my nose. A faint perfume memory lingered, and from that I gained strength. Perhaps my mother had chosen the talisman with more care than I had imagined. She would, of course, have known that the perfume would be strongest at the time I missed her the most. But it would fade as time passed and finally I would be forced to face the world with only a memory of its fragrance.

'Hello Marcelino, and how are you today?'

'I am well, my friend. And how are you?'

'I too am well. And where are you going?'

'I am going to the town by the sea.'

'Can I join you on your journey?'

'I would be glad of the company.'

A part of my past had caught up and now fell into step with me. I had earned my name again. I had paid for it with the memory of the loneliness I had felt that night in Pamplona. There would be other difficult times in the days ahead, but I knew my strength was returning as I came once more to the outskirts of the town by the sea.

12

This area of the town was unfamiliar to me. The streets were narrow, the alleys crowded with dwellings. The impression was that the countryside around it had begun to encroach on this district, because in some of the yards I passed there were cows and horses. Hens clucked and scratched at the cobbles, in a yard a pig basked in the sun in a pool of its own filth. I continued, lost in the reasons for my journey. And only then did it come to me: if I returned to the place where I had begun, perhaps I could find the woman from the tower again. I was sure that there was something that had tied us together when first I encountered her in her shop. But this time I would be more cautious. I would set out my case and throw myself upon her mercy. The kindness I had detected in her would, I was now sure, prevail. I would tell her my name and, if there was nothing else I could offer her, perhaps she would acknowledge that I was honest and begged no more of her than a few moments of understanding.

And so I walked towards the sea, crossing the thoroughfare of shops, past the museum, along the streets of small cottages and out on to the promenade. The sky was by now a single shade of gauzed blue, as if a net had been hung across it because the blueness itself was too vivid to bear. Rain threatened. The sea was a gently chopping grey. No boats were visible. There was nobody on the beach. The tower lay ahead of me and I was soon back at the shelter which bore the initials of the town's council. Here I rested, this time taking the seat which faced the woman's shop.

The shop door was open but was too distant to see whether she was inside. Beside the door, the sails of a paper windmill were turning quickly in the breeze, the friction of the paper against the wooden stick making the sound of a minute engine. The thin stick was planted in a bucket of sand; the wind was straining its back a little. As I watched the windmill, I became hypnotised by it, imagining something of the journey which had brought it there: the dusty, dark workshop where it had been made by a man with poor eyes. I could see his bench and I could see the green visor which he wore on his forehead. I could discern his patience and I knew, simply by looking at the windmill, that the man had no children of his own but had taken to making the toys for the children of the world. He compensated himself for his loss by imagining their enjoyment. It was a single red windmill. Red, because in some way it took him back to a windmill in his childhood, and although the windmill had not been that colour, it was the colour he saw in his mind whenever he thought of it. He was living in his past, and I entered it and stood with him for a while.

When I left the toymaker's world, the woman was at the door of her shop, looking out to sea. She had, I knew, not seen me in the shelter because I could tell that she was unaware of being observed. She, too, was lost in memories as she leaned against the frame of the door, her arms crossed against her breasts, the breeze toying with her hair. I saw her open her mouth wide as if in a silent scream and then take a long draught of the breeze. She held it within herself before expelling it. When she had done so, the dullness in her expression was gone and she was alert and anxious for distraction. It was at this moment that I raised myself from the bench and she saw me.

I did not approach her. If she had shown alarm, I would have walked away. It was not my intention to frighten her. I allowed her some moments to become used to my presence before, slowly, I crossed the road and stood in front of her. The woman appraised me with fresh eyes, testing what she now saw against the memory she held of me. But I also sensed that she had recently learned something about me because her expression showed an amusement I had not previously seen. I faced her in the knowledge that if we were to communicate with each other, it would not be through a shared language. Happily, the will was there. The woman smiled at me in a manner I knew was intended to convey reassurance. I smiled in return and with some formality offered my hand to her. She took it and shook it and let it fall.

At that moment I remembered that I did have something to offer her which I had misplaced before: I could give her my name, which is often the only thing of value we can offer to strangers. What they choose to do with it dictates how that friendship progresses, whether it becomes the title of a new book they write in their hearts, or simply a scribble on a scrap of paper which is let loose in the breeze the moment we have parted.

'My name is Marcelino Merida,' I said, touching my palm to my chest to make myself as clearly understood as I could.

'Marcelino,' the woman repeated. I was sure we were on the verge of a greater understanding, but at that moment there was a sudden commotion in the street behind me: a dog barking, men running, men shouting. The woman's alarm was immediate. She took my arm and drew me into the shop. Once inside, she pushed the door shut, drew a bolt and peered through the glass towards the street. Beyond her, I could see a number of men passing her door. Some had sticks and cudgels, one restrained a panting dog which tugged at its leash. Following on behind them, after a moment's pause, came Pinch and Duke, and Duke's malodorous mastiff. The woman watched the men go by and then allowed a further moment to pass before she turned her attention back to me, marooned in the centre of her shop. She leaned back against the door and smiled. There followed an indeterminate period of confusion and stalled understandings.

The time passed quickly. I was a visitor in the woman's world and therefore, initially, felt obliged to take the submissive role when such difficulties arose. But I quickly came to see that she despised what she viewed as weakness. When I stood up to her, the arguments were fierce but they burned brightly and quickly; after each one we saw each other more clearly and found new ways to navigate the world we were constructing together. It was, like all joint endeavours, an exhausting process. The negotiations over how much each of us should give and take were often protracted. But this was for the good. The foundations we were building were solid. Instinctively, we understood that we would each best serve the other by remaining true to ourselves. I learned that the woman had, indeed, once been married, that her husband was gone, and that she was not sorry to have lost him. It seemed that the women he had known before her had all accepted his expectations of them and had been moulded by them. It was because they had given in to him that he despised and abandoned them. When he met the woman from the shop, a basket over her arm, walking prettily along the promenade, he had fallen in love with her immediately. They had quickly married and moved into the shop she had been left by her father. For a while, like the women before her, she had complied with his instructions, but although she was young, she soon came to understand that to make him happy she was losing herself.

One day she caught a glimpse of herself in the glass of the shop door. She was wearing a dress she would never have chosen for herself. Her eyes were dead. She was exhausted, despite sleeping for twelve hours a day. She visited the doctor, who diagnosed unhappiness. He told her that the only cure lay in honesty and openness. Her husband would understand, he assured her. Ultimately they would both find the necessary strength to carry them forward.

They parted two weeks later. Her husband, who had lived with her for three years, packed his clothes and left the town. The woman remained, exhausted and unhappy; her anger was now directed towards the doctor. Perhaps, she conjectured, she should have listened more to her husband; the weakness may have lain with him. They could have worked together to understand each other a little more. The doctor agreed with her that she should not now dwell on the parting. There is profound happiness to be found in life, he told her, and it often lies on the other side of misery. She would soon be glad of his advice, but she must not turn away from her unhappiness. He would help her to confront it. In doing so, he comforted her on many occasions. He visited her during the day and night. Some nights he stayed with her. He lost some of the respect he had earned in the community when he was seen in the mornings walking back to his surgery. People accused him of being a selfish man who had cost the woman her marriage because he had always, secretly, been in love with her.

But the woman knew the truth. She was a passionate woman, and she enjoyed the passion of the doctor. He stayed with her because she asked him to. There was no shame in that. She was a free woman. He was a free man.

Several months after the woman's husband had left, a woman in the shop asked her why she did not marry the doctor. She told her that she had no business asking such a question. But the answer, had she given it, would have been that, as a prospect, the doctor was considerably less promising than her husband had been. Although he had diagnosed her condition, he was blind to his own short-comings. This, she knew, was often the case with men who were quick to offer sympathy or understanding. Such feminine traits, she recognised, were, in a man's clumsy hands, weapons more effective than brute strength. On the night the doctor asked her to marry him, she told him not to visit her again.

Since then he had taken to drink and was often found asleep at dawn on one of the town's damp benches. His patients no longer called on him at night. His judgment was seen to be lacking in difficult cases. He rarely attended births. When he pronounced the death of a patient, the relatives tended to seek a second opinion. It was only his older patients who continued to wait in his surgery. The elderly prefer fallibility to change.

It was tragic, the woman declared, that a man could fall in such a way. But she felt a responsibility for the doctor's predicament. Their situations now reversed, she took it upon herself to visit him. She would call on the doctor at the end of the day and make sure he ate a good meal. Because there was rarely food in the doctor's house, she would be sure to bring the food herself. And she would not allow him to drink wine as he ate and she ate with him. Under her care, his strength returned. So much so that, one evening, he declared himself fit and well. He raised himself from his chair after the meal, made his way over to the armchair beside the fire, lit his pipe and asked the woman to take the other chair. He had something to tell her, something he only now understood. It was this.

When she had first come to see him, he had immediately discerned the reason for her unhappiness, but had genuinely believed that she and her husband could come to some accommodation. For any marriage to survive, it is necessary for both partners to endure a blunting of some part of their natural inclinations. In her case, this had gone too far and, to balance it, a simple adjustment was now required on her husband's behalf. Once that had happened then, with luck, a new equilibrium would prevail in which the woman could reclaim something of herself. He stood by this diagnosis, and argued that it was she rather than he who had chosen to end the marriage. When, however, he began to visit her at night, and then stayed in her bed, he found himself questioning his motives. The woman was rare, he well knew, in declaring that she wanted nothing from him beyond their nightly companionship. She revelled in the physical nature of their relationship as much as he did; it was she who reassured him that nothing untoward was taking place. But, like a priest, a doctor must act like a man while not exhibiting the feelings of a man. He had failed in this regard by showing desire for this woman, and this led him to believe he had failed many of the women he treated. Too many of them visited him in his dreams. He maintained the pretence that it did not influence the decisions he made, but clearly it did. Like a fallen priest he was flawed. And until he had reached an age in which desire had passed him by, he would always be at its mercy.

'I understand this now,' the doctor told the woman that night as they sat, one at each side of the fire. 'Thank you for leading me towards this understanding.' They embraced. The woman returned home, glad that the doctor was now at peace and that her job was at an end.

Within a few days the doctor was seen to be drinking again. He was, however, never incapacitated by it. He had, it seemed, found a level of medication for himself which enabled him to go about his daily life with the pain of his imperfections in check.

Her experiences with her husband and the doctor had, therefore, made the woman wary of any future relationship. This was the history I contended with. As for me, my instincts were similar, although I could not quite as clearly have explained my reticence to her. Cause and effect, in the woman's world, were important in removing the complications of her life. Once she had experienced the effect, she would not rest until she had arrived at what she considered to be the cause. When I suggested to her that life was not so simple, she argued that my position was without authority; and what I failed to understand was that whether or not the cause was the correct one, the greater importance as far as she was concerned was that it was good enough for her: if it satisfied her, then I should accept it. But in doing this, I would argue, she missed an opportunity for a greater understanding of herself. In return, she would claim that she asked for no greater understanding. What she craved was what we all crave: contentment. And if there is an element of misunderstanding at the root of that, then so be it. That is all very well, I would suggest, but if we are to build a relationship, then we must both subscribe to these beliefs.

And so the arguments would go on. The truth was . . .

. . . The truth was that we held no such conversations. How could we when we spoke not a single word of each other's language? Time did indeed pass quickly, but it was an hour and no longer that I spent in her shop. She was kind to me. She asked me to eat with her, and I gratefully accepted. But she did not ask me to share her bed, and when I had eaten and had conveyed my gratitude, she led me to the door of the shop, undid the bolts, and I went out into the cold night.

Afterwards, I sat on the bench in the promenade shelter and watched the lights of the shop go out. It was here that she came to me, fully written; her story, her life, her hopes. Soon after, the lights went out in the tower. The woman was alone with her dreams, and alive in mine.

13

I awoke on the bench the following dawn to the cry of the gulls, remembering the last battle.

It was some weeks after the night in the garden of death (when the fool visited the sleeping men and slit their throats). We had been marching for days that had seemed endless, occasionally pausing to confront the resistance to our advance on Madrid. I recall trying to concentrate on the orders being issued to us, but I was losing the fight with my exhaustion. It seemed, from what we were being told, that the advance on the city would begin in a little under an hour's time, at seven a.m. We were to advance through Casa de Campo towards the north-west edge of Western Park. At this point there was a moment's lapse in my concentration as my chin dropped forward. When I came alive again I heard: '. . . ford the river to the north of the bridge, south of the railway, continuing the advance through the Western Park in order to occupy first the Model prison and the Infante Don Juan Barracks . . .'

Since I had left Burgos I had seen so much that had

terrified me that my mind now felt broken, often questioning the direct evidence of my eyes. This dislocation set in when I stood back and watched my compatriots fighting in hand-to-hand battles in the trenches outside Talavera. With horror I saw a man biting off the ear of another man and spitting the blood-edged pellet of flesh to the ground. When I turned away I was confronted by the sight of a huge Moor who, roaring with laughter, was pushing the eye of the young militiaman he was murdering out of its socket. Later I saw a mixed band of artillerymen and Legionnaires scavenging among the Republican corpses and forcing open their jaws in the search for gold teeth. Bone, I learned, cracks like stone, not wood. But in Talavera it was demonstrated to me that when men go to war and their humanity is threatened they find strength within themselves, an old strength that comes from instinct, which lies beyond wisdom. I saw nobody die without putting up a fight for life, except for those caught unawares (the Legionnaires in the overgrown garden at Illescas seemed to accept the tender release of death from the fool who knelt across them with his knife).

That final night in Illescas changed my fortunes. When I awoke in the silent garden the following morning it was a surprise to discover that none of the Legionnaires had stirred. I raised my head and looked around me for the fool, but there was no sign of him or of his kit and rifle.

Some instinct, something in the quality of the silence, held me back from sitting up and stretching. It had been many weeks since I had lost the habit of rushing out at dawn to meet the new day. Like my mother I had become cautious, wary of the traps life might have set during the night. I consoled myself that at least I had found an ally in the fool. Although the man exhausted me, he did provide companionship. I had become tired of being excluded by the circles of men, unsure where to get my tin plate filled with food, anxious about taking too much from the pot.

When the murder of the Legionnaires was discovered and the alarm raised, the news spread through the column not with sadness or fear or anger but with relief. Death had visited and filled his quota; those he had not chosen to take with him considered they had good reason to believe they would survive the battles to come. Of all the men, the Moroccans were the most superstitious, and because I was the only one in the garden to survive the slaughter, I found myself being approached by them to act as their talisman. I was courted respectfully. First, around the middle of the morning, two men – elders – approached me as I sheltered in the shade of the wall. They presented me with an accordion which had been owned by one of the slaughtered Legionnaires. The mice which lived inside it were already nosing through a tear in the bellows for food. Later, early in the afternoon, a senior officer came to squat on his heels beside me whereupon he handed me a shiny pistol in a smart leather holster. Because I could only communicate with these huge men by nods and gestures, I imagined I was being given an opportunity to buy the weapon. I pulled my empty pockets inside out and shrugged to indicate that I had no money, but the man pressed the pistol into my hands. He then patted me on the shoulder and ruffled my hair. A group of men were watching to see how I would respond to these overtures. Of course I embraced them eagerly, much to the disapproval of my fellow-volunteers who had not been singled out for such attention. When I was formally transferred from the *requetés* to the Third Tabor of the Regulars of Tetuán, it was without any regret on either side.

To mark my transfer I was given my first rudimentary instruction in firing a rifle. Finding the weapon too heavy for me, I decided to try out the pistol I had been presented with. The gun was attached by a lanyard to the holster, and when I drew it, for the first time I felt like a soldier. Away from my new friends I practised drawing the weapon. But on the one occasion I did loose off a shot the recoil startled me so much that I determined to use the pistol solely for decorative purposes.

I woke again, the pistol snugly at my side, to find the briefing over and men in the column standing and saluting as Lieutenant Colonel Asensio moved among us. I saw the drivers and artillerymen going to the trucks, the smoke belch from lurching exhausts as the cold engines were started. The Legionnaires and the Moroccans gathered up their kit and smoked their final cigarettes, preparing themselves for the march to Casa de Campo. I wandered in a daze around the circus of men and vehicles. An artilleryman sitting in the back of a truck recognised that I was lost and offered me his hand; I found myself being tugged up into the air to sit beside him. The men of the first column were confident of victory. They had marched and conquered for seventy kilometres to reach this point and now only the river and a few thousand ill-equipped *madrileños* stood between them and the heart of Madrid.

I did not share their confidence. I prayed and thought of my mother and tried to picture the cathedral at Burgos. But I could find nothing to calm my fear. My lungs felt swollen with terror. My breathing was so shallow and rapid that I felt light-headed. I searched the horizon for some fresh image to carry with me into the battle but everything I saw, from the burned-out church to the bullet-pitted trees, was scarred by war.

As we approached the lines, the activity intensified. Men were clamouring around a wireless. I heard: 'People of Spain! Put your eyes, your will, your fists at the service of Madrid.

Accompany your brothers with faith, with courage, send your possessions, and if you have nothing else, offer us your prayers. Here in Madrid is the universal frontier that separates Liberty and Slavery. It is here in Madrid that two incompatible civilisations undertake their great struggle: love against hate; peace against war; the fraternity of Christ against the tyranny of the Church.'

A truck passed us, followed by an ambulance ringing a bell. Three men cycled past, rifles slung over their shoulders. A column of men untarnished by war were waiting by the road. They looked fresh, their equipment new, metal helmets hanging from their belts. The river was close by. And then we were in the din . . .

It was a din so loud that, even with my fingers pressed into my ears, I could still hear it. I felt utterly without purpose, the more so being surrounded by men who were so expert and drilled for this moment. It was evident to all of them that this was what they had been put into the world to do. They fired their rifles as they ran, they dived to the ground, they crouched, they moved forward with stealth, they looked for cover. Moors, Legionnaires, all seemed instinctively to know what was demanded of them. I stumbled in terror between them until a hand tugged me to the ground and a huge ugly mouth tried to scream some sense into my face. Men moved to the left and right of me on the flank. Commands were shouted. Rifles called. Bang,

bang, bang! The noise of a blacksmith hammering a horse-shoe inside my head. The artillery was a deeper din. Heavy shells were being lobbed over our heads towards the forces crouching behind the boulders in the north of the park. It seemed ludicrous that such angry destruction could be taking place in such a beautiful, peaceful setting. Trenches had been cut under the scrub oak trees. The river lay just beyond. A short distance away, men were sheltering behind blocks of concrete and firing at us. Others fired from trenches. There were sticks of fire. Deep thumps of bombs. Fizzing fuses.

Cowering behind a tree, I prayed for the fool to find me. The fool would know what to do. The advance had already moved past me. Men were clambering out of trenches and greeting them and they were embracing and dancing. Why would they dance? Perhaps they had seen sense or perhaps this whole war had been staged for my benefit. I swore I would gladly live by the lessons, if only I could understand what those lessons were. But the men who danced together were soon tumbling to the ground. When they had rolled together in the mud, only one of them would stand up again, stained by the blood of his partner. He would not be smiling, or bowing, or thanking his partner for the dance.

I heard a truck behind me; as it slowly passed me I grabbed the tailgate and hauled myself into the back. Inside, there was the stench of diesel from an open can and a clutter of wooden shell crates split open; shiny metal shells rolled loose, two bottles of wine were wedged in the netting, three backpacks were stacked like corpses. The owners of the packs, the artillerymen, marched behind, using the truck for cover, holding on to the lorry. I picked up a rifle and set it between my knees. It ticked like a pendulum as we moved. The truck embarked on a slight gradient; I leaned out and saw the sky above me. At last there was something clean, as if a cloth had wiped away the scribbles of the aircraft and left the new sun and the blue canvas behind it.

The gulls continued to cry as they flew across the canvas of my new world. I was grateful for their cries. However insistent their din, it would not issue a shell or a shard of hot metal. Nevertheless, after lying on the bench for a time and listening to the bickering in the skies above me, I found my patience tried. I left the bench and moved from the proximity of the woman's shop along the promenade and towards the heart of the old town. The rusted metal fingers of the clock on a church indicated that it was shortly after 6.20 a.m. My limbs loosened the further I went. I felt the need for the sea upon my body and descended the damp steps which led from the promenade to the beach. The ones closest to the sand were green with slime and treacherous.

Standing upon the sand, I imagined that the steps continued below the level of the beach and that the changes in the tide exposed a greater or lesser number of them. I found myself caught up in contemplation of the invisible steps and resolved that, should I settle in the town by the sea, one day I would return to the beach with a shovel, dig down, and discover how many steps there were beneath the sand.

I took a gentle stroll towards the line of the tide which carried above it its own gentle chill. It rushed to greet me then pulled back again, repeating its eternal tease. I paused to remove my boots and set them neatly down, one beside the other. On top of these I deposited my clothes, and then I approached the water. Before I reached it, I paused. I would let the tide come to me, happy to join the game it was playing. While I waited, I clenched my toes and made indentations in the sand; the grit abraded the hard skin of my toes. I claimed the beach and the beach claimed me. The thin tide rushed to me and broke with a sweet, freezing sharpness over my feet. The chill spread up my legs and body and rested about my neck and shoulders. I luxuriated in it as I took a step forward, then another and another, so that when the tide next approached me it lapped against my shins. With four further steps I was in the permanent water. Behind me, the tide continued to go about its game.

At the point where my walk became a wade, I paused

again. The chill of the water continued to signal itself. A
body roused from sleep is barely alive. The only true wake-
fulness is brought about by the shocking embrace of cold
water. I plunged forward and struck out towards the horizon.
The icy water sent a charge through my body. When it
reached my head, it passed away with a shudder having stolen
my warmth. The waves were gentle; nevertheless I felt the
tug of a current drawing me away from the shore. I took
a mouthful of water and spat it out. The vile taste of the
salt remained. The chill grew in strength the further I travelled away from the shore. When I paused and lay on my
back, kicking my feet for buoyancy, I looked along the line
of my body and could see beyond my toes the dwarf of
my clothes in the far distance. Behind them, above the line
of the promenade, I saw the full extent of the town: a line
of low buildings like a row of even teeth, the exception
being the tower which rose high into the clouds. To the east
of it there were further shops; beyond them what I assumed
to be other houses, similar to the one the doctor inhabited.
There was a pleasing symmetry about the vista. But the
town's length soon shortened; my clothes no longer visible.
The change in perspective had been caused by the current
pulling me further out into the open sea. I felt like a drunk
in the arms of a fellow trying to help me to my feet. The
waves were higher. The town disappeared momentarily, reap-
pearing again when the grey wall of water fell. For the first

time I was afraid. Since I had arrived in that place I had eaten very little, which I knew had weakened me. I pushed my arms out ahead of me and dragged them wide, hauling myself through the water. What little progress I achieved was lost when the next wave carried me effortlessly away from the town again. I struck out once more, three strokes, four, five, this time using as much strength as I could muster. I did make progress, but it cost me a great deal of my strength, and while I rested, again such progress as I had made was lost to me.

Perhaps, I considered as I turned again on to my back to conserve my strength, my time was at an end. I prayed that wherever I came to rest on the shore, it would be a place where a stranger would receive the charity of a decent burial.

So be it. If this was to be my fate, then why waste the last of my life fighting to preserve it? Instead, I could lie on this hammock of waves and watch the sky and contemplate my life and prepare to meet my maker. This I did and was visited by a peace such as I have perhaps only once found in my life. If life is a simple struggle for sustenance and, beyond that, for meaning, I had no further need for sustenance and strove no more for understanding. My mind cleared and I felt a warmth rise up inside me. My body demanded sleep, and although I resisted it, finally the pull was too strong and I succumbed.

14

On waking, I was first aware of the warmth of the air. I felt as if I lay in a womb, so perfect was the temperature. I was afraid that if I moved a muscle, this would be lost to me and so I lay, still and silent, until a familiar voice roused me from my slumbers:

'Marcelino! . . . Marcelino!'

I opened an eye to a sky bleached by the sun. To a red sail; to a rope stretched taut to a mast; to a man standing at the prow of a skiff, his hand grasping the rope for support. The sea rose and fell. I could see him only in silhouette because the sun was behind him, but I was in no doubt that I was again in the company of the fool.

'See? He wakes.' The fool turned and told the sea.

I was lying on a folded sail. The fool reached down and took my hand and pulled me up to a sitting position. I was light-headed and felt as though I had been sleeping for days. I had none of the aches and anxieties of life upon me. I was there, on the boat with the fool, the sun ahead of us, the sea around us, and we were at sail on an ocean of peace.

The fool knelt and, from a basket, tugged out a bottle wrapped in straw. He removed the cork with his teeth and I took the bottle from him. The water was cold. The route it took through my body came alive with the shock of it. I took another draught and handed it back gratefully. The fool now crouched upon his heel.

'I was afraid for you,' he said. I had never seen him so sober; indeed had doubted that he had the capability of such sobriety. But I saw that he was addressing the bottle, not me. He cradled it in his arms and laid it once more in the basket.

I had questions, but they could wait. My ignorance contributed greatly to the peace I was feeling. The wind carried us on. The fool made an address to the wind and the sea.

'And where are you taking us?' he wanted to know. 'To Heaven or to Hell? Will you see us through the storms that approach or will you cast us into the depths? And how will you treat my friend: will you save him for another time or will our fates be the same? Does he want to survive or does he want to perish? Will you allow him to make that choice for himself? Survive or perish?'

The whisper of the sea against the shore roused me although its voice seemed to be pleading for silence. The fool was gone but the peace I had experienced remained. I was lying on the damp sand having been deposited there by the tide. I could see black shapes swimming in the shallows. When I got close to them I discovered them to be my clothes enlivened by the air trapped within them. I claimed them and dressed. I looked towards the horizon and then turned back to face the town. I felt there was little I did not know about this place now. I knew it and it knew me. In the pocket of my jacket were a number of coins the woman had pressed into my hand when I left her. I would find a place to eat and then I would seek out the doctor. I have endured many days with fewer ambitions.

I approached the counter of the coffee house I had first entered with Pinch and Duke. A woman waited there for me to reach her, her hands preparing to busy themselves upon my instruction. By now I had accepted that any communication would be difficult and so had already determined I would make my preferences known by gesture. A man was breakfasting close to the counter, his plate laden with eggs and bread. I smiled at the woman in an attempt to assure her that I was not an imbecile, and then laid the coins upon the counter to establish that I was not a vagrant. Her expression remained uncertain. She seemed lacking in the generosity of spirit which would have predisposed her towards a stranger. Instead she wore the suspicious, malevolent glare I had come to recognise as characteristic of this place. I had not conformed to the usual practices and was therefore owed her suspicion. Wishing to conclude my dealings as quickly as I could, I nodded towards the man with the plate of eggs, attempting to convey to the woman that this was to be my choice of breakfast. I did it in such a way as to suggest she should not bring my choice to the attention of the man at the table. I did not want him drawn into the transaction. But the woman had no interest in propriety and immediately called out to the man, interrupting his gruesome, open-mouthed consumption of the eggs. While he listened to her, his mouth remained open, revealing strings of yellow yolk falling from the roof of his mouth and pooling on his tongue. He drew in air through his nose. When the woman ceased talking to him, he resumed his eating; it seemed he was capable of only one task at a time. His eyes were blank. A habitual state, I imagined, and one shared by the woman.

The man went back to his meal and the woman barked some shrill question at me, allowing me to understand that I had provoked her anger. I gestured that I did not understand. She barked again, this time looking towards the coins on the counter as if she was drawing them into her complicity. I heard the man's knife and fork being laid heavily upon the table and a grunt from him to her to convey some reassurance that the attitude she had exhibited was the appropriate one. I had not gone there with the intention of annoying the woman, indeed I had adopted a position of deference, imagining that this would predispose the woman towards me. But it was hopeless. Whether or not she understood what I was asking her (and I suspected that she did), she had chosen to make my position as uncomfortable as she could.

I tried once more. Now that the man had been invited by the woman into our conversation, I considered I had an equivalent right to his services. I therefore walked to his table, picked up his plate, showed it to the woman, pointed towards the coins on the counter and returned the plate to the table. While I watched the woman to establish whether she would understand me, I felt the man's right hand anchor itself upon my forearm. I tried to pull away, but the man was strong. He stood, maintaining the pressure of his hold upon me. Seeing the woman's face, it was clear that any help I might have expected from her would not be forthcoming. She spoke to the man, offering him reassurance; she then looked on as he dragged me by my collar from the coffee house and into the street outside. I looked vainly behind me as we passed the counter, hoping at the very least that I could retrieve my coins, but the woman had already collected them and I saw her slipping them into a pocket of her apron.

Once outside, the man released me. I took a wary pace

away from him, and then backed away a little further. A woman paused to watch. She was joined by a boy and a girl before others collected around them, sensing a show of violence. The man was adding to their expectations by tugging up his sleeves to reveal quite huge forearms. A wide ridge of vein travelled along each one, disappearing beneath the man's shirt cuffs. He was soon playing to the crowd, bouncing upon the soles of his feet, thumbing his nose and adopting the stance of a bare-knuckle fighter. I stood quite still and watched him as he danced around me. Surely he would not strike out until I too had adopted his stance? And I had every intention of prolonging this moment for as long as I could.

The woman from the coffee house came to stand at her door. I tried to plead with her one final time but she would not acknowledge that she had met my eye. I did, however, see a glimpse of her shame before she masked it; it confirmed what I had already deduced: that decency existed somewhere within her, just as it exists within us all.

A fist flailed towards me but was pulled up just short of my nose. I neither flinched nor moved. The fellow was setting his distance before the punishment began. I stepped away from him. A voice called encouragement. There was the sound of a horn as a motor car signalled for the crowd to make a way for it. By now the numbers had swollen to such an extent that the road was blocked. How word had spread so quickly I do not know. The motor car travelled away, and I think I was the only one who watched it go but, as I did, there was a darkening in my vision. Immediately a huge weight connected with my cheek and my head was consumed by a red bursting pain which exploded across my eyes. Yellow messengers of agony flew about my body, fleeing as fast as they could from the site of the pain. I staggered backwards a step, hearing the crowd as if they had taken up residence in an echoing chamber. The street had become a mirage shimmering beneath the sun. Ahead of this mirage, looming large and quite solid, the fellow bounced upon his heels. This dance was for the benefit of the crowd, to recapture their interest in him now that it had transferred itself to me. Having struck me and been unrewarded by any show of retribution, the fellow was less certain of his position. He would lose the sympathy of the crowd if they perceived the beating to be too brutal or unjust. His nose came close to mine, then away, then close again. I could smell his rank breath. The site of the pain felt soft and full of blood. I tested the inside of my cheek with my tongue. Another fist was launched towards my head.

This time I ducked, although I was not conscious of having made the decision to do so. The fellow's arm flew above me, his weight carried him on, and as I stepped aside I saw him collapse on the pavement behind me. This drew a rousing cheer from the onlookers. Could it be, I considered, that they were cheering his misfortune? Were they offering their support to me? The hope this gave to me raised my spirits so swiftly that I shook my head to clear it of the agony. I would put up a fight against this bully. I would make these people grateful for my presence among them. I would fight to belong.

I turned to face the man as he lifted himself to his feet. He rose like a huge beast requiring its entire strength merely to stand. He glowered. For him there was now no crowd around us; no longer was he fighting for approval but for honour, and such rules of conduct as he had chosen to abide by were dismissed. A flurry of angry blows rained upon my head. I can liken it only to an experience I had as a child when I chanced into a cave of bats. Having disturbed them, they flew about me, shrieking, and then, as one, were gone. I am tempted to liken the bats to a cloud, but in truth it was like being assailed by a net of snapping fish. The ferocity of the blows about my head was such that I felt as though I was observing the assault from above my head. I threw up my hands to defend myself but they were pushed aside by the battering. Sparks of pain filled my head, the colours of the world became muted and mixed. My head connected with the ground and the pain of it distracted me momentarily from my concerns for my face and teeth.

There was nothing within my field of vision but the floating sky. I tried to close my ears to the sounds of the street. The fellow loomed over me. He leered. He pulled back his boot and he applied it with some force to my side. A second kick was arrested by a call from the crowd and he walked away. With effort I lifted my head from the ground and, from that low angle, saw him enter the coffee house. The woman from the counter allowed him to pass her before she followed him in. There was a blissful moment of peace before she emerged again and approached me. From some misguided sense of politeness I tried to stand, but could only sit. She held out her right hand, gesturing that I should also hold out mine. Into it she dropped the coins she had taken from me. Her expression was sober and without malice now. Perhaps, for decency to take root in her, it would be necessary for her to witness a series of such unwarranted beatings. Cruelty conditions us far more effectively than kindness.

In the moments that followed, as I attempted to regain sufficient strength to stand and rid my head of the din of pain, I could see that the crowd had not entirely disbanded. Although none seemed inclined to approach me, some discussion seemed to be taking place as to whether I should be offered any assistance. I had imagined that only a victory over the fellow would have won them over, whereas the injustice of the attack seemed to have had a similar effect.

But as the debate continued, and as I drew in a number of breaths to steady myself, I found a figure standing above me, blocking the sun from my face. When I looked up I saw that the man was familiar. He held out his hand and I took it and he pulled me cautiously to my feet.

15

It was the doctor, the friend (or lover, or perhaps no acquaintance at all) of the woman from the shop. Although I recognised him immediately, he differed from the image I had preserved of him in my mind. He was shorter and older, his body squarer. Having seen him only briefly, I had not registered that the man had a white beard which was trimmed short to his square jaw. His moustache was yellow above his lip, the symptom of his cigarette habit. A short nub was fixed in his mouth now, the red coal glowing to signal each drawn breath. He was wearing a dark, loosely cut suit, a white shirt and a narrow black tie. On his head was a dark hat with a wide brim. His apparel suggested that he had a personal sense of formal style, though his clothes could not be said to have been new or in any way fashionable. He carried a wooden stick and I discerned a slight limp as he encouraged me to take a cautious step to test my strength. When I had done this we both looked down at my legs as if they had been taken outside from a shop into the daylight and I had tried them before the purchase was concluded. As the look we exchanged readily acknowledged, they had served their purpose. I had done well to come by such a fine pair of limbs. If, at that point, we had shaken hands and he had walked away, I would have been grateful for the kindness he had shown. He had no debt of care to me. However, he remained in close proximity, anticipating, perhaps, some after-effect of the beating. His being a doctor, I imagined he had encountered such a situation before, and so we stood, as if waiting for a parcel to arrive or for some other party to join us. Both of us watched the end of the road as we stood in silence.

During this time, the doctor took out his cigarette case, unclipped it, and slipped a cigarette from the band which held them fast. He tapped the end of it on the closed case and applied it to the darkened channel between his moist lips from which he had removed the previous one. He then lit it with a flint lighter and enjoyed a deep draw of smoke. His clothes had been tainted by his habit to such an extent that, even standing some distance away from him, the smell was considerable. The aroma of damp straw was not, however, entirely unpleasant.

When we had waited long enough, the doctor led off. I hesitated, uncertain whether I was to follow, but he turned and, by his expression, beckoned me on. I chose not to walk beside him but fell into step behind him. He seemed content at this for he did not slow and allow me to catch up with him. I sensed I was in the presence of a man who needed no reassurance from others and expected those who walked with him to feel the same. He knew exactly what shadow he cast in the world. He greeted nobody (although he must have known many of the townsfolk) and nobody greeted him. It was a brisk walk and soon he was at his door. I waited some distance away from him as he opened it, climbed the single step and went inside. I knew I could not simply follow him in, but contemplated what form the invitation would take. I did not want to provoke his impatience by appearing too timid and holding back, equally I did not want to seem too bold and simply stride in after him. After all, which way would he turn? Would we find ourselves sitting awkwardly in the surgery, as if in some consultation, or would he lead me into the quarters at the back of the house, perhaps to the kitchen? I would have preferred the former. I no more wanted to see the doctor's kitchen than I would have liked to see the man in his shirtsleeves. The image I had built in my mind was that of a formal gentleman, a man untrammelled by domesticity, and it was important for this to be preserved.

In the event, as I waited and pondered, the answer came quickly and it was not one I had foreseen. The door was slammed shut.

I could only suppose by this that the doctor had waited for me to enter behind him and had lost patience when I did not. A man does not slam his door without good reason. It is a signal to the world that the world should remain beyond that door. So far as the doctor was concerned, I was the world's representative and he had effectively closed the door in my face. But knowing the man as I now did, I recognised that this was merely a challenge, and that we had therefore reached a significant point in our relationship. He would have known well enough that I would not simply have walked away at this slight. Indeed, I doubted he would have seen it as a slight, rather a sealing of our new friendship. The more I considered it, the more convinced I became. The slamming of the door was, in fact, an invitation to me to throw open the door and walk in. This was the kind of man he was: a fellow with strong feelings and opinions, impatient with the niceties he saw around him. He had greeted nobody in the town because he had no desire to conduct a conversation with anyone he passed. The townsfolk, I expect, had long ago accepted this of him. And if he seemed a little brusque, it was not rudeness, for rudeness is an intended departure from the individual's habitual behaviour. It seemed almost ludicrous now to have contemplated him inviting me in in any other way. Would such a fellow stand on the step and wag a finger in my direction? Would he cough coyly, shyly step aside, and allow me to lead him across his own threshold? No. He would slam the door in my face. Even now, he would be removing his coat, settling in his chair and waiting for me to join him.

'So there you are,' is all he would say when I walked into his parlour or surgery. 'What took you so long?'

On such firm foundations, our friendship would be built.

However . . . I had taken a step towards the door when another consideration crossed my mind. Would he not see it as a sign of weakness if I immediately complied with his expectations by answering his call to follow him in? Perhaps only a meek fellow, hungry for companionship, would make such a move. And while, after witnessing the fight, I did not imagine that he would have considered me weak, perhaps there was sufficient doubt remaining in his mind that he wished to test me. And if this was the case, then I should not enter his door. Instead I should either wait outside, or, best, simply walk away. If he was watching me, as I suspect he was, and I was proven right by choosing the latter course of action, he would signal this by throwing open the door (or window) and inviting me in. Whether I should accept this invitation, I would judge when it had been made.

There was, therefore, no other course of action but to turn and walk away. As I did so, I sensed his eyes upon me. But how long would he wait before calling out? I took one step after another, the coins jingling in my pocket like the bells of distant goats. I had reached the end of the terrace when I began to wonder if I had misinterpreted the fellow, for no signal had been forthcoming from him. But perhaps not. If the doctor had, as I suspected, chosen to test our friendship by these means, anticipating that I would understand and accept the terms of this test, he might well regard this as the final stage. Knowing what he expected of me, and what I expected of him, I now knew that I had no choice but to turn the corner without looking back – for looking back would be an acknowledgment that I antici- pated he would be waiting and watching. I sensed him expending a grateful breath as I turned the corner and was lost to his sight. Breathing heavily with the exertion myself, I leaned against a wall. The test had exhausted me, but I had undoubtedly triumphed.

When my heart had returned to its normal lilting beat, I stood straight again, and took charge of my weight. The doctor would be back in his chair; coffee would have been called for from his housekeeper, and he would be waiting for me to return and enter his house without knocking.

I admit to a failing of nerve as I faced the doctor's door for a second time. The window was sufficiently close that with one step to my right I could have peered into the surgery, but that would have been the very worst thing to have done. I doubted that he would have been watching me return along the street although I walked as though he was — with firm strides, head held high. I could do little about my torn clothes and the blood and bruising on my face but the smile I carried, I hoped, was sufficiently well constructed to indicate that it mattered little to me. Turning the cold handle of the doctor's front door, I walked in and closed it firmly behind me.

Blindfolded, I would have known this to be the doctor's residence from the smell of tobacco smoke alone. The hallway was dim; all of the doors which gave on to it were shut. I paused briefly but knew I could not hesitate for too long. To the right of me, I knew, was the entrance to his surgery. Beyond it was a further door to the back parlour — ahead, the one to the back of the house. A stairway on the left rose up to the first floor and, tucked behind it, a further set of stairs which led down to the basement. I walked past the door to the surgery, instinct drawing me towards the back parlour. I tried the handle, gave a gentle knock, as politeness dictated, and pushed. But the door was locked.

The barrier of the locked door emptied my reservoir of certainty. My time in the town by the sea had rendered me fragile. I needed longer before I could regain sufficient confidence to face the doctor. But I did not want to flee the house. If I had done so, I would not have returned. The staircase to the upper floor seemed as great an obstacle as the closed doors. The one which led to the basement was the only route I felt confident enough to take.

It was not long into my descent of the stairs that the aroma of the doctor's stale smoke was overwhelmed by a sweeter, ranker smell of damp and rot. My memory prompted me that I had first encountered it when I entered the tower. It had emanated from what I had imagined to be the storeroom. The smell was quite overpowering and demanded so much of my attention that I soon put behind me my other fears. I held my sleeve to my face, the contact of the cloth against my nose offering some comfort.

The foot of the stairs was in darkness, but my eyes greedily drew some illumination from the whitewash on the cellar walls. By this I could see that the floor was orange brick. Coal was piled in drifts against the walls in three wooden stalls. In another bay, on a mat of sacking, there was a pile of muddy potatoes. Several rusting tins were stacked on a crude shelf which truncated at an opening in a wall. Beyond it was another dark recess. I felt the grit of the coal on my soles as I went towards it but stopped dead when I heard footsteps crossing the floor above me. In the silence I felt my heart leaping with terror. I could not be discovered here. Who else but a common thief would be cowering in a cellar?

The boards above my head creaked against their nails as they bore the weight of the doctor's tread. I heard the sharp scrape of a chair and perhaps (although I might have fancied it) a cough or a clearing of the throat. I pictured the doctor

176

settling into his seat and shaking out his newspaper. He would tear it a little with the force he employed; he had lost patience waiting for his visitor. The stories in the press would try his patience in a way they would not have done had I simply taken my courage in my hands, knocked on his surgery door, entered, and shaken my new friend firmly by the hand. But the playing of such games requires considerable finesse, the duration of the contest being significant. By settling to his newspaper, the doctor was indicating to me that the game was at an end and I had failed. I could only hope that the connection between us was now severed. I did not want him in my mind, seeing the cellar through my eyes. He lit a cigarette. The smoke fell between the gaps in the floorboards and permeated the air around me.

I contemplated how long I should wait before climbing the stairs and attempting to leave the house without the doctor hearing me. There was no reason to delay, but, despite my shame, I remained curious about what lay beyond the opening in the wall. Perhaps I would learn something about the doctor's life by discovering what he stored in his cellar.

The rear chamber was much larger than the one I had first entered. Undoubtedly it extended beyond the house. The walls, again, were brick and washed in white. There were a number of pieces of furniture about the floor, but I remained curious as to what was hidden in the shadows which lay like sacking shrouding the far wall. There had been no further sounds from the room above, so I continued across the chamber and was soon cloaked by the darkness. It was not so complete as to render me completely blind, rather it was the final degree of grey before one can call it black. But such a level of illumination plays tricks with the eyes. As they strain for purchase, the scant information they serve to the mind sends it scurrying towards memories. A tree, for example, encountered this way, can be rendered by the mind as a horse up on its hind legs; low, solid objects as holes through which one could fall. And everything in this twilight world becomes sinister; the darker memories belong to the night and the terrors one has felt in one's dreams. I reached out my hands ahead of me and continued to take one careful step after another. I expected, soon, to reach the far wall, and the further I went, the more the anticipation of any contact became unbearable. But the wall did not come. Five, six, seven further steps and still it had not come. There was no illumination now and I realised with horror that I had become disorientated. I did not have the confidence that, should I turn, I would be able to retrace my steps. I had no choice but to proceed and hope that I was walking sufficiently straight that I would not circle the cellar for the rest of time. I went a little faster, the fear of colliding with something now less great than that of being marooned for ever in the darkness.

When I arrived at the wall I hit it with such force that I fell and lay sprawled on the floor, comets of blue light racing through my mind. Standing, I was afraid that I had lost the wall, for I could not immediately find it when I reached out. But I was facing the wrong direction, and, by turning, gained some reassurance from the feel of the cold, damp brickwork.

It was, however, a small reassurance. Although the discovery of such a solid boundary had been my sole objective, I had already forgotten the reason why. Tracing the wall, however, would eventually lead me back to the first chamber. Hand over hand I felt my way along the bricks. They seemed to be covered by residue; each one I touched sent a small shower of dust falling over my feet. When my fingers touched metal it was so unexpected that the shock of the contact made me recoil as though I had put my hand in a flame.

It was a door, and I had no difficulty in opening it. I could immediately hear the sea, distantly calling. I could see a corridor stretching ahead of me. Light and water spilled down into it from recesses above. The floor was submerged beneath a rapid stream of water which flowed away down the slight gradient. I closed the metal door and stepped into the current.

179

16

The water was cold. As I stepped into it, it reached up above my knees. I stumbled as I fought the current, which urged me to hurry along at its own pace. Resisting the pull, I reached out to take hold of a ridge in the damp wall. The water broke against the back of my thighs. I tested my strength against it and paused for a moment before choosing which direction to take. But there was no choice to be made; I had no strength to fight against the current. The world I had entered had a strange kind of beauty, the more so because it was hidden from the people of the town. Light dappled the brickwork around me; the music of the water was broken by the gentle splashes of the rats which scurried along the ledges and occasionally dropped into the flow.

I released my hold on the ridge and proceeded along the tunnel by the light from above. Every few steps I reached out to take hold of the wall to reassure myself that, should I need it, it was still there. After some minutes I reached a fork in the tunnel and chose to take the route to the right. The floor was a step higher, the stream here a tributary that flowed slower. Here the air was less rank and soon the breadth of the water I walked in narrowed until it had become nothing more than a trickling channel, the brick-work of the walls dry. Above me I could hear the voices of people gathered together. I paused to listen. There was some laughter, voices raised in good-natured argument, but the mood of the gathering seemed genial enough so I cast around for some access to the ground above me. I walked on, and it was only when the voices were some way behind me that I came upon a ladder. It was anchored firmly to the wall and reached high into a vertical, circular tunnel above me; this chimney was some twenty feet high and at the top of it a circle of light was capped by a grid of metal. I climbed the chimney, which was a little wider than my shoulders, and when I reached the grating I pushed at it with my head. It was hinged and opened like a trapdoor. Soon I was once more out into the light.

It was only when I turned and saw the tower behind me that I knew I was on the eastern edge of the town. I was standing in a road which bordered a large field. The grass had been freshly mown. On the field were pitched a number of tents and among them were roundabouts and wooden galleries, swing-boats and tall towers topped by painted bells. At the feet of these towers, men swung hammers, landing them upon anvils which sent bullets of metal careering up the tower towards the bells.

I was soon among them and found my spirits lifted by their proximity. I enjoyed watching their endeavours and smiled a greeting when any face found mine. As I wandered between the stalls, my thoughts turned to the doctor and how I could solve the riddle that our friendship had become. It seemed cowardly to have left him in such a way. I felt guilty that I had been the cause of his ill humour.

Something drew me towards a boy with his mother. They were standing together, quite close, watching a man trying his strength. Neither the woman nor the boy was enjoying the spectacle. Although the woman smiled as the fellow spat on his hands and grasped the long shank of the hammer, it was with anxiety. In the time I had been watching them, the man had made three swings at the anvil, but he was not strong and the metal bullet had leaped no more than halfway up the tower. The second swing achieved even less. By the third he was so weakened that the bullet went no more than a foot before dropping back. The woman, who was minding the man's jacket, folded carefully over her arm, made a step forward and took the man's sleeve. She was trying to lead him away towards the roundabouts, gesturing at the boy as though it was for the boy's sake that they should move on. The young boy, however, was loyally watching his father and making no demands on him. Perhaps it was the lack of such demands that impelled the father to ignore the woman and take hold of the hammer once more. His wish was to present his son with the simple gift of the ringing of the bell; a father's strength is a son's strength until he inherits his own. But so is his weakness, and the man sensed that others were watching him now; perhaps there were some boys who knew his son, and could see what his father was enduring. They would take the easiest comfort — which is to clothe oneself in the discomfort of others.

The fellow handed another coin to the man who minded the stall. From the way he received it, it was evident that he could not have cared less where his income came from, although I suspect he occasionally flattered the men who rang the bell by telling them how rare were such feats. The woman's look towards him was imploring him to refuse the coin. The boy's concern was being transmitted entirely through the mother. With all my heart, as I stood watching the woman clutching the sleeve of her husband's jacket, then reaching out to draw the boy towards her, I willed the man to find the strength to ring the bell. And by now the crowd, it seemed, had the same hope in their hearts. The women were viewing the scene through the mother's eyes, the men entirely through their own. And the children watched either because the adults were so rapt at the scene or because, being a little older, they saw an opportunity to witness an adult demonstrating his folly.

The man drew in a breath and took a firmer hold on

the shank of the hammer. However, before he lifted it and took on its weight, he turned and looked around and saw the crowd that had gathered behind him. He must also have seen his son, and indeed his wife, because the fierce concentration on his face was wiped clean and confusion took its place. I am glad to say that, as is rarely the case, the prayers of the mother and the son were answered, because the man found the strength to hand the hammer back to the stall-holder and walk away. Taking his jacket from his wife, he slung it over his shoulder with such panache that one could have been forgiven for believing that he had succeeded at his task. I watched them as the crowd parted and the man, his left arm now linked with the woman's, his right arm around his son's shoulders, went off towards the roundabouts.

Such moments provide so much hope that I long to share them with Commissioner Ruis. Because he was not too proud to hide his tears, he made me understand what it is to be human. And it was to the Commissioner I turned when I returned from the war after an absence of three years.

17

The journey home had been long. I was impatient to see my mother. And when I arrived in Burgos, I tore up the Calle de Alcalá, my arms outstretched like a bird. The night pursued me, but candles in the windows held it at bay. With each step I shed the past three years like layers of clothes; already I felt lighter and stronger. With each step I became younger still. On I went as the sun dropped away and I was through the door before the dark could catch up with me. Up the six flights of stairs I ran and sat breathless and red-faced at the table waiting for my mother to set the dish in front of me. This is how I had imagined it would be. I would be there, at her table, without any word of warning, and she would come out of the small kitchen and see me, and I would say, 'What, Mother? Have you prepared nothing for your son?'

I was home at last and, sitting alone at the table, listening to the sounds from the kitchen as the meal was prepared. We would have defeated the world, my mother and I. Together we had that strength. And, even on those days when I sat beside her bed and she could not face the light of day, we would still draw strength from each other. Even when those days became weeks, we remained resolute in our strength. I learned to hide the beatings from my mother, for I know she felt the pain of them more strongly than I.

And so I waited at the table while my mother busied herself with the meal. I did not recognise the dish she was preparing; the smell was unfamiliar to me. When I looked around the room I saw that it had changed. The walls had been scoured of their relics. The furniture was old. There were crumbs on the table, an unwashed plate on the floor. A bed, standing against the wall where a chair had been, was unmade, the filthy sheet hanging down to the filthy floor. My mother had become ill. There was surely no other explanation. I pushed the fear away to the corner of my mind. If she was ill then I was back and could look after her. I resolved never to leave her again.

The figure that emerged from the kitchen was a slow, ugly creature. It was an old man. His eyes were poor; he looked towards me and then peered closer to establish that I was real and not a ghost at his table or a figure conjured by the shadows. My chair clattered to the floor as I stood and fled.

Dashing through the night I soon reached the house of Commissioner Ruis. Gold light blazed from the windows. I hammered on the door and waited, panting, as I listened to the slow footsteps of his man approach the door and draw back the bolts. The man had never had any patience with me. He saw my visits as unwarranted intrusions into the life of his master and would try to send me away. But that night he could see I would not be so easily repelled. He stood aside and I pushed past him and found the Commissioner alone in his chair beside the fire. He rose as I approached him, as though he had been expecting me. We embraced and when I tried to pull away he would not let me go. By this I knew that my mother was dead.

The Commissioner and his man looked after me in the days that followed. I was feverish. When I woke from dreams I found myself in other dreams, in old places and memories, in happier times when I walked through the fish market at dawn and the women called out to me; when I played with the children before they tormented me; when I sat with my mother, long into the evenings, and we would talk of my life and what the future held. Slowly I adjusted to my new circumstances, and when the fever had passed and I said goodbye to the Commissioner I knew I would never see him again.

I glimpsed the fool (it could have been the fool or someone who looked quite like him) when I walked away from the Commissioner's house. I saw him dart into an alley, and I followed him. Beyond the alley was a road; one road led to another, and as the days wore on I walked miles until I found myself in the city of wood (where the buglers sailed out on metal tracks). After this city came another. I took a train and another train and a boat and then, early one morning, I awoke on the beach of the town by the sea and the story of my life to this point comes to an end.

When I turned back towards the fair and its garish distractions I saw a face that was familiar to me. Although I could not immediately place it, I knew the associations were strong and good. I felt a warmth about my heart and my pulse beating faster. I was captured by the beauty of the woman's face, by her demeanour, by the slenderness of her neck, the delicacy of the smile she employed on those who stood around her. She was allowing them to pay court to her, but her expression suggested that she would, without hesitation, withdraw the favour of her attention if something displeased her. It was the woman I had encountered at the auction and had travelled with in the carriage. I stepped back into the crowd, anxious to preserve the distance between us. For as long as this remained, there was the possibility that everything would be healed between us, that we could find once more in each other what we had found in that journey through the night. I watched her and even though I did not enjoy the way she teased the men who surrounded her, I could bear it because I knew that I had been closer to her than they.

I followed them to a shooting gallery which the woman reached first. She paused to indicate that it would please her to partake in the attraction. There was some commotion as the three men in the group vied for who was to pay, which would of course have bought them the right to guide the woman's finger to the trigger, to steady her arm, to hold her shoulders tight so that the barrel would be directed towards the target. But this was the moment I chose to make my move. As the men fumbled in their pockets and coins showered to the floor, I strode quickly towards the group, covering the distance in a very short time, and was soon standing between the woman and the three men. The good humour of the group was extinguished. They knew of me, that much was clear. A stranger would not have provoked such a fierce and sudden hatred. But there was only one whose reaction mattered to me. Regrettably, she turned away to hide her face from mine. And while she composed herself, the three men arranged themselves in such a way as to block my path to her. I did not try to barge through them but waited for her to turn towards me again. The men could see that I was resolute, for none of them tried to push me away or strike me. They had all folded their arms, one after the other, which made them seem more comic than threatening. She finally did turn and stare towards me through this wall of brawn. There was no bravado on her face. In fact there was nothing at all. I do not believe I had ever seen her face so naked of intent. Should I have read shame or fear, regret or hope? I knew, however, that her expression mirrored my own. We had known each other for such a short time that we had made no contract between us. We had parted in that rare and precious period before any demands are made.

One of the fellows chose to speak at this point. He tossed a comment over his shoulder to the woman, asking her for instruction. She did not answer immediately. I don't believe she heard him because, like me, she was reliving that journey in the coach, hoping that the answer to her predicament lay there. Receiving no reply, the fellow turned around to face her. He was dumbstruck that the woman had not responded, never having known her to exhibit anything but certainty. Her attention continued to be directed entirely towards me, which meant that I saw the moment she made her choice. She smiled, very briefly, but then she became sly. To her credit, she chose to turn and walk away, drawing the others in her wake, before she passed comment on me. And their response to what she had chosen to say was half-hearted. When they had been swallowed by the crowd I felt no real regret because it was the brief smile that I will carry in my heart; the knowledge that our liaison had mattered to her and she would carry the memory of it for the rest of her life.

I felt the familiar sadness again, that which prefigures

each departure. But this time, although I knew the time to leave had arrived, I had few regrets. I was leaving without having been defeated and on my own terms, my dignity intact. If I so chose, I could return to the town by the sea without shame.

But how should I depart? There would be a clue. And it came as no surprise to me to see, at that moment, Duke roaming through the crowd. I noticed him because he was carrying a glass jar which was suspended from his raised hand like a lantern. His full attention was concentrated on the goldfish inside the jar; the crowds parted to let him pass through. Some distance behind him the mastiff followed on a slack leash. I knew that Pinch would be close by, and because I was enjoying the novelty of being the spy rather than spied upon, I chose to follow Duke as he made his way through the fair.

Pinch was waiting for him behind a tent. I stood in the shadows and watched as Duke reached him and immediately handed him the jar. Pinch held the fish up to the sun as if, by doing this, he could see through it. It seemed to have satisfied him because, when he let it down again, he patted Duke on the shoulder. Duke tried to hide the gratification he had drawn from this but his face wore a smile as the two men, the fish and the dog removed themselves from the fair. I followed them at a distance, curious as to where they were going.

193

At one point Duke stopped and looked behind him; whether this was because his senses were sharp and he knew he was being followed, or whether it was out of habit, I do not know, but I was so far behind them that he did not see me. We were still on the eastern side of the town and walking in a direction that was taking us towards the sea. The breeze was chasing inland from the shore. Pinch and Duke bantered eagerly like the newest of friends; the dog followed them like an old memory. At the approach of another man I saw Pinch stiffen, but the man passed them by without comment. When they turned down a road with a public house on it, they stopped just short of it. After peering towards the building for some time, they made a dash past it and did not slow until it was some way behind them. The dog tore along after them. Later, Pinch paused at the window of a clothes shop and pointed eagerly through the window towards an item he wanted to bring to Duke's attention. Duke expressed an opinion that seemed to find favour and they moved on again. Finally, they reached the old harbour gates and I followed them through the boatyard. At the far end, beyond those rotting hulks which had no hope of repair, they took a set of wooden steps down on to a pontoon and walked along the rocking surface towards the far end where an old green fishing boat was tied up. Duke climbed aboard first. Pinch followed, and the mastiff dropped into it soon after and lay, waiting on the deck, while the two men made their way inside the wheelhouse. Remaining on the harbour wall, I looked down on them.

Because they did not emerge I drew a little closer and saw them both looking into a large fishtank which ran half the width of the wheelhouse. The tank contained goldfish which darted about one another, much to the amusement of the two men. They took turns to point and bring to the attention of the other the antics of the fish.

Having discovered the lair of Pinch and Duke, any menace I had felt from them, any hold I had imagined they had over me, was gone. Their boat, the goldfish, the sleeping mastiff conjured a scene of happy domesticity. They sought no company; indeed, I believe they saw the world around them solely as a source of unwelcome distraction. I envied them but was also angered by them. I have the arrogance to believe that I can have a place in anybody's life if I so choose.

When I am alone and I explore the root of my beliefs, I find that I owe them all to my mother. In her disdain for the world she created in me an elevated sense of my own worth. I have lately come to question whether this may be misguided (and I see no contradiction in this from the other, profound belief that I am undeserving of the space I take up in the world). As a child I was, after all, a contradiction – both my mother's shame: a fatherless child; and her joy: her only son. I now believe that my mother disparaged the world because it saw only her shame and turned its back on her. People regarded her as bitter but they did not have the privilege of knowing her as I did. I became her surrogate in the world and inherited the disdain people felt for her. It was a burden I never complained of. Commissioner Ruis once expressed admiration for this. I explained to him that it was not a matter of choice but of duty and he understood me a little better although I know that it puzzled him. My mother had been a handsome woman. Men saw in her an availability. I overheard them praising her body and the promises her eyes made to them. But she could not help being imprisoned in an unsuitable body, and I believe in the long days of her despair it was this that troubled her most – which was why she locked herself away.

For many months after her death I regretted that I had not had the opportunity to say goodbye to her, to thank her for her love. But I now know that she said goodbye to me when she pushed the perfumed cloth into my hand as I boarded the lorry for Pamplona. Unlike the perfume, her love for me does not fade.

I had been standing for some time by the harbour wall lost in my own thoughts. When I heard the sound of an engine starting I looked down again towards the fishing boat. Duke was now on the pontoon, loosening the ropes which tied it up. Pinch was in the engine house, standing at the wheel. The mastiff stood alert, his nose straining into the wind. Whether they were leaving the town for good I did not know but I knew I must go with them. I called to Duke and he saw me and shouted to Pinch who looked up in my direction through the window of the wheelhouse. When Duke jumped on board Pinch came out on to the deck and beckoned for me to go down and join them.

If I had seen something pass between them to make me doubt that their offer was genuine, I would have walked away. But I discerned no snide intention in the gesture, and so I took the steps down to the pontoon and stood beside the fishing boat. Untied, it was moving slowly away, although the engine was idling. Without waiting for a second invitation I jumped aboard. The mastiff barked and backed away. Pinch looked at Duke and then he held out his hand to me. I took it and we shook hands, and I did the same with Duke. Pinch then returned to the wheelhouse, the engine rose in pitch and the fishing boat was soon navigating the alley of vessels on its way out of the harbour. I sat on the aft deck looking back towards the town. From the low angle, all I could see were the tops of some of the taller buildings proceeding past, and of course the tower.

We ran out past the harbour arm and into the gentle swell of the sea. By now the town was laid out before us. In the company of the two men, who stood shoulder to shoulder in the wheelhouse, I felt more alone than I had when I had only myself for company, but I did not regret having accepted their offer.

A final thought came to me as the tower slipped from view beneath the horizon. It was that we are all of us happy, but some of us are also unhappy. I was grateful to have left some of the burden of my unhappiness behind me in that town by the sea.